Published by Inhabit Media Inc.

www.inhabitmedia.com

Inhabit Media Inc. (Iqaluit) P.O. Box 11125, Iqaluit, Nunavut, X0A 1H0

Photography: CRP/Shutterstock.com, goldnetz/Shutterstock.com, eAlisa/Shutterstock.com,
Piotr Krzeslak/Shutterstock.com, Espen Solvik Kristiansen/Shutterstock.com, Stas Malyarevsky/
Shutterstock.com, Vishnevskiy Vasily/Shutterstock.com

Editors: Neil Christopher, Kelly Ward, Grace Shaw, and Kathleen Keenan
Art director: Danny Christopher

We acknowledge the support of the Canada Council for the Arts for our publishing program.

This project was made possible in part by the Government of Canada.

Printed in Canada

Library and Archives Canada Cataloguing in Publication

Title: Taaqtumi : an anthology of Arctic horror stories / compiled by Neil Christopher.
Names: Christopher, Neil, 1972- editor.
Identifiers: Canadiana 20190138149 | ISBN 9781772272147 (softcover)
Subjects: CSH: Horror tales, Canadian (English)—Canada, Northern. | CSH: Short
stories, Canadian
    (English)—Canada, Northern.
Classification: LCC PS8323.H67 T33 2019 | DDC C813/.08738089719—dc23

TAAQTUMI

An Anthology of Arctic Horror Stories

Compiled by
Neil Christopher

INHABIT
MEDIA

Contents

Iqsinaqtutalik Piqtuq:
The Haunted Blizzard

Aviaq Johnston

THE WIND BLOWS WITHOUT MERCY AGAINST THE BUILDING, making the students chatter with excitement. We ignore the teacher and run to the big, turquoise-trimmed windows. Looking outside, we see the telltale signs of a blizzard: the growing snowdrifts, the snow blowing across the ground, people struggling to walk against the wind. We also see—well, *don't* see is more accurate—other signs of the blizzard. Buildings and landmarks missing on the horizon as the approaching storm obscures them in its white and violent embrace.

There is a high-pitched *beep*, then the PA system crackles as the voice of the school secretary comes out alternating languages from Inuktitut to English. "Due to the sudden change in weather, school is cancelled until further notice. For students with older siblings at the high school, you must wait to be picked up before leaving. Please notify a parent or guardian once you arrive safely at home!"

Anything that our teacher may have said is lost as all thirty of us exclaim in delight and rush out of the classroom to get our jackets on and leave. Within moments, I am bundled up into my

1

snow pants, my winter boots, and the parka my auntie made for me this year.

A stampede of students storms out of the school from all exits. I am among the grade sevens, the last grade before we move on to the high school uptown. We are at that age where we are old enough to leave the school on our own, even if we have a sibling at the high school.

We burst from the recess door where a playground is protected by the u-shape of the school's courtyard. We usually call it the kindergarten playground because it is safer and easier for teachers to watch as they shiver in their Canada Goose parkas. The day is already darkening, as we barely have sunlight for more than a couple hours in the winter. A twilight has taken its place in the sky.

The playground is nearly abandoned as the younger kids in lower grades wait inside for their parents or siblings to pick them up, and other older kids leave through other exits with more direct paths home. We older kids run in haphazard directions, excited to go home to do whatever we want: watch TV without parental or sibling intervention, eat all the snacks left in the fridge or cupboards, sneak around to see what our parents might be hiding in their bedrooms.

The wind blows sharp snow pellets against my face. It stings my eyes, but my body is filled with such jubilance that I don't care. Ulii, Nita, and I all run toward our section of town together. We live near the breakwater on the shoreline, the *iksarvik*. Our houses are all close enough together that we can get most of the way home before splitting up.

Ulii is the first to separate. Her brother is smoking a cigarette on their porch, bundled into a shabby coat. He must be freezing.

He isn't wearing gloves or mitts, and as Ulii arrives at the steps, we can hear him berating her for no reason, as he always does.

The storm continues to thicken as Nita and I keep trudging home. We stopped running just outside the playground, our excitement dwindling, and we are now leaning forward into the wind. Our heads are turned to the ground, our hands holding onto the fur trim of our hoods to keep the wind from blowing them off our heads. We slide from the middle of the road where the wind is strongest to walkways between houses where there is more cover.

We reach Nita's house next. Its humble frame is surrounded by hunting equipment strewn across the ground. The equipment had been tied onto her grandfather's *qamutiik*, but the wind has loosened the grip of the rope, and the tools are being swept away. Her grandfather's husky is bundled into a ball on the porch to stay warm.

Nita's grandmother is staring out the window, waiting for her arrival. Once she spots us outside, she rushes to open the door.

"*Atii, tuavi!*" she calls out in Inuktitut. She can't speak English. "Come on, hurry up!" is what she said.

Nita rushes up the stairs and I continue on my way home, but her grandmother calls out to me again. "Inu!" she calls. "Stay with us! It's too dangerous . . . this storm is full of bad things!"

"I'm okay, Grandmother!" I answer in Inuktitut. Having grown up copying Nita, I call her Grandmother, too. "I will be home soon!" I tell her.

She keeps calling after me, but I've gone too far. The wind distorts and carries her words away.

I walk around a mound of snow built up by snowplows. The wind rests for a second, and I finally look up from the path I know by heart. I can see my house from here, elevated a metre off the ground on stilts drilled deep into the permafrost.

In the fleeting quiet, something feels wrong. I stop walking for a moment and look at the path ahead of me. Everything seems normal. I look behind, and there's nothing—

Wait.

There's a shadow.

Something squeals from my throat and I start running. The wind soon picks up speed and sharpens, piercing my ears as I run.

I remember what Nita's grandmother shouted at me, and I want to kick myself for not listening. Her voice echoes in my mind. *This storm is full of bad things.*

There are blizzards all year long. Sometimes they come only once a month, but often they come more frequently. Sometimes they destroy things in town, blow the doors and roofs off buildings, cover tracks in the snow that hunters need to follow on their way home, and bury precious equipment until the snow melts in the summer.

This blizzard is different though. Elders tell us stories about blizzards all the time, about their danger and about the things they do to our homes and our people. Once in a while in Inuktitut class, an elder will tell us about a storm that fits itself in among the others. Once in a long time—years and decades in between—this blizzard comes back. It roams through our land, bringing something with it. The elders never tell us what it brings; ghosts or creatures or perhaps it is simply the shadow that I caught a glimpse of in that second. They just say to find shelter and to never be alone.

This storm is full of bad things. She had tried to warn me.

I am running, but barely moving. The path behind my house

feels like it's turning into a tunnel as the wind picks up again, and I'm fighting against the air.

I hazard another look back, and the shadow is still there. It looks like a person. It's following me, but the wind is slowing it down, too.

Finally I am close enough that I can touch the side of my house. Reaching the stairs, my feet finally have traction and I climb up the steps as quickly as I can. I lock the door as I make it inside, flicking on the porch light.

A gust of wind howls up the stairs outside. There are no windows in the porch, so I can't see if the shadow has followed me here. I'm too scared to move as I lean against the door, hoping the lock and my weight can keep me safe and secure. The house is empty and dark.

Ring! Ring! Ring!

The phone rings from the living room. I'm still stuck in the porch, frozen.

What was it?

The phone keeps ringing until the answering machine picks it up. After the beep, I hear my mother's voice. "*Panik?* Call me when you get home, okay? I'm stuck at work. The weather is too bad outside."

My mom's voice makes me feel safe again, so I head to the living room still wearing all my outdoor clothing. I flick on each light I pass: the hallway, the kitchen, the living room.

I dial my mom's office number. She answers on the first ring. "Panik?" she says.

"Hi *Anaana*," I say.

"Are you home?" she asks, but she gives me no time to answer because she already knows I'm home. She saw our phone number on the caller ID. "Inu, are you alone? *Ataata* is going to try to get home, but he has to wait for everyone to leave so he can lock up at work."

"Yeah, I'm alone." I tell her.

"Okay," she says. The wind is booming against the house. It's getting harder to hear her voice. "You have to stay inside; it's too dangerous. I already heard that the roof of the Northern is being blown off."

"Yup. Anaana?"

"Huh?" Anaana says, her relief at knowing I'm home safe has changed her apprehension to disinterest.

"I think I saw something when I was coming here," I say frantically. "There was a shadow and—"

"It was just someone trying to walk home in the blizzard, Inu." My mom's voice sounds frustrated. She sighs. "You and your imagination."

"I really saw it!" I say.

"*Taima*. That's enough." Her frustration thickens in her voice. "I'm already worried as it is. Ataata will be home soon."

"Okay," I say, but my stomach is sinking into my knees and my chest feels like it is being pushed down and squeezed tight. "Bye."

"I love you, Panik," she says before she hangs up the phone, all the way at the other end of our island town.

My mother doesn't know. She's too grown up to remember the scary parts of our land. The scary things that hide around us. She thinks that the land is nothing more than the science of the space around us, environment and nature. She thinks this is all that lives outside.

For some reason, elders and children know more than adults do, and I wonder why that is. They act like they know everything, as if everything has an explanation. At some point in their lives they forget the stories children are told, dismissing them as fairy tales and myths. They think that the scary women in the ice aren't real, or that the little folk that you can only see at sunset are just imaginary, or that giants never roamed the earth. Just like all adults, my mother has forgotten all those things the elders had passed down.

But . . . maybe it does make sense that it was just another person walking home in the blizzard. *Maybe* that makes sense.

I may have been confused. In my memory, I see a tall human-shaped figure, with long limbs, long hair, made entirely of blackness, of shadow.

But maybe my mom is right.

With my growing calm, I decide that my mom was probably right. My dad will be home soon anyway, and if adults are too blind to see the scary things around us, then maybe the scary things can't see adults either.

I turn on the TV and sit on the floor. Kids cartoons come on the screen. I don't even like them, but I don't want to change the channel. The cartoon is full of bright and vibrant colours, and I am beginning to forget the shadows I have seen.

Before long, the blizzard winds tear against the house, and suddenly, I am in darkness.

Power outage.

In the quiet I notice something. Utter silence. The wind outside isn't booming anymore. Through the open curtains I can see the gusting wind, but I can't hear its howling cries. In the silence, I notice a different sound emerge. A small, yet frantic sound. A clinking from somewhere inside the house.

Slowly, the sound of the wind picks back up and the small sound is lost in the noise.

Something seems wrong again. The hair stands up on the back of my neck and I look around, trying to find where the clinking noise is coming from. But I can't.

I look back to the TV and see myself reflected in the dim light coming through the window. The kitchen is visible in the TV's reflection as well, and for a moment I don't pay attention to it. The electricity always goes out for a bit during a blizzard. It's normal enough. I look back at the TV, willing it to turn back on. . . .

Until I realize that there is a shape in the kitchen window. A shadow peering in.

The power comes back on, the lights shining bright as they return. Slowly, I look back to the kitchen window, but I don't see anything. I stand up and walk toward the hallway.

I look back at the door, brow furrowed and heart racing. For a moment, I don't seem to know what is wrong as I look at the dark porch. The winds are blowing as loud as ever, the noise deafening, but normal.

But . . .

Didn't I turn on the porch light?

I feel the breath catch in my throat, no more air coming in or out. I scream and run down the hall to my parents' bedroom, the farthest from the porch.

The door to their room is open and I am about to run straight inside, but something catches my attention. Staring past the room, to the back door that we never use, something is different about it. It's been closed and locked shut for years.

The doorknob is shaking, turning back and forth with urgency. That was the frantic little noise I had heard when the power was out. Whatever is outside, it is trying to come in through the door.

I am stranded. Maybe there is more than one of what I've seen, at both the door and the window? And somehow it turned off the porch light?

So . . . is it already inside?

I turn around and run toward the one bathroom in my house. There are no windows in there and it is the only room inside the house that locks. I slam the door shut, locking it.

But when I turn away from the door and see the shower curtain drawn, my heart stops. Neither I nor my parents ever leave the shower curtain splayed across the tub. Tears fall freely from my eyes.

I am stuck.

Truthfully, I don't know why I'm crying, sobbing, screaming in such terror. I don't know why the shower curtain is scaring me so. I don't know what hides on the other side.

Darkness extends out from behind the curtain, it dims the light to almost nothing. The wind is shaking my house violently, as if in a hurricane, a tornado, a flood, an avalanche. I can't see anything in the darkness, I can just feel the floor shaking beneath me as I crumple down, trembling as hard as the shaking house.

A voice I have never heard before speaks, scratchy and hoarse, "*Qanuikkavit?*" it says. "What's wrong?"

"*Anigit! Avani!*" I cry into its darkness. "Get out! Go away!"

A laugh echoes out, "*Qanuikkavit?*" It keeps asking.

There is a scratching noise, metal against metal, as the shower curtain is pushed aside.

The Door

Ann R. Loverock

THE DOOR STOOD ALONE AGAINST THE BACKDROP OF THE tundra. It was white, almost lost in the endless field of snow. The only thing that stood out was the black doorknob. Joamie blinked hard. He turned off his snowmobile, threw his shotgun over his shoulder, and approached cautiously. Up close it looked like any regular door, except that it was standing alone in the middle of the Arctic. He gently touched the sides, sliding his hand underneath to feel the space between the door and the ground—it wasn't attached. He shivered and took a step back.

"What in God's name?" he said.

Joamie had left his house that morning at roughly six a.m. It was springtime. The sun had just begun to peek over the horizon, giving him a precious few hours of light. He was hunting polar bear, although he would bag a wolf if he saw one: the Northwest Territories Hunters and Trappers Association offered $150 for the pelts, and he could use the money. But after nearly two hours, Joamie had managed to kill only one Arctic hare. *Not much*, he thought. *But better than going back empty-handed.* The daylight had already begun to fade. He had skinned the animal with his knife and put the red flesh in a plastic bag. After securing his catch to the back of his snowmobile, he'd driven off toward the village.

And then he'd seen it.

As Joamie stared at the door, he noticed the world around him had grown eerily quiet. Usually the wind was stinging his face, but it had stopped blowing. Everything around him was silent, unmoving. Without knowing how it happened, Joamie found his hand on the doorknob. A bad taste formed in his mouth, and his stomach was in knots. He fought hard against the urge to open the door. He had a feeling deep in his gut that this was something unnatural. Something evil. He used all his willpower to remove his hand and ran back to his snowmobile. He took off for home without looking back.

He arrived home, breathless and shaken, just as the darkness took over and hurried into the house with his catch. His grandmother, Ethel, was sitting at the table sewing beads onto a moosehide jacket. Joamie stood in the kitchen, snow falling off him in heaps that melted into puddles on the floor.

"Take off your snowsuit in the entrance," Ethel said.

Joamie went into the kitchen, threw the hare into the sink, and went back to hang up his clothes to dry. When he came back, his grandmother was filling a pot with water. She could tell from the look on her grandson's face that he was upset.

"I found something," Joamie said.

Ethel waited for him to continue speaking, but he just stared at her, his eyes wide.

"What?" she said finally.

"I couldn't bring it back with me. It's not something . . . I have ever seen before. I mean I've seen one before, but not like this."

"You're talking crazy. What did you see?" Ethel asked.

"There was a . . . a door. It was just there all of a sudden. It looked like it was floating."

Ethel looked at Joamie askance. What he said sounded insane. He expected her to laugh or cry because her grandson had lost his mind. He noticed her body stiffen. She stood for a moment, unmoving, as though she were transfixed.

"Did you touch it?" she asked.

Joamie nodded. "Just lightly."

"Did you open it?"

"No. But I . . . I wanted to."

Joamie stared intensely at his grandmother. Her face was contorted in fear. He had never seen her look like that before. She spoke slowly, in a hushed voice.

"Joamie, you must not open that door. You understand? If you see it again, you do not open it."

"Where did it come from? Why did I see it?"

"I don't know."

"What happens if I open it?"

"Listen to me, Joamie. You leave it alone if you ever see it again. That's all we're going to say about it."

Ethel shook her head and turned away. She took out a bag of flour and began busying herself. "Do you want some bannock with dinner?"

"Gran? I . . ."

"Joamie, stop!"

Joamie sat down at the kitchen table, swallowing his questions along with his fear. "Yes, you should make some bannock. Maybe take out the jam too," he said.

Ethel smiled and began to hum. "We need to go to church this Sunday. We haven't been in a while. I saw Father Gagnon at NorthernMart. He told me we have been missed."

Joamie nodded his head in agreement. His grandmother had been a practising Catholic since missionaries had arrived in the village when she was a child.

"I guess we should go this weekend," he said. "You're one of the most respected elders in the community. You have to set an example."

Joamie couldn't help but think her sudden urge to go to church had something to do with the mysterious door. The sickly feeling swirled in his stomach and crawled up into his throat. He swallowed some water and tried to stifle it, forcing it back down. He ate his dinner in silence and went to bed early.

Joamie did his best to forget about the door. Allowed it to fall into the deep recesses of his mind where he had shoved other bad memories, like the time he was beaten almost unconscious by Jackson Bishop, the local bully. Or the image of his mother lying in a casket, her face calm as though she were sleeping. Joamie did his best to keep all his darkest memories buried. Ever since his encounter with the door, he hadn't been able to keep them out of his mind. They kept bubbling up to the surface, jolting him awake, heart pounding.

The weather changed, and with warmer temperatures came the midnight sun and the best season for hunting. Nearly half the village would spend time harvesting muskox, bison, and caribou.

Early one morning, Joamie's neighbour Darrell arrived at the door carrying a shotgun. Darrell was a little older than Joamie, in his mid-thirties, but looked closer to fifty. His skin was weathered and cracked, and he had deep bags under his eyes. "Joamie, we're heading west to hunt for caribou tomorrow. Why don't you join us? We got a small group together. Going for maybe two or three days. We could use you."

Normally, Joamie would jump at the offer, but the swirling nausea in his stomach gave him pause. He looked at his grandmother for approval. She was standing behind him with her arms crossed over her chest.

"You're not going to get better weather than this," she said, motioning to the sky. "We need to eat."

Darrell smiled and gave Joamie a friendly slap on the shoulder. "Get your survival gear together. I'll swing by tomorrow. Early."

Joamie went to sleep feeling anxious. He tossed and turned, dreaming about the door. In his dream, he was standing in front of it, trying to stop himself from opening it. It was like his hand had a mind of its own. He couldn't stop himself from turning the knob. The door opened to blackness, a deep, dark abyss that Joamie felt himself being sucked into. It felt sinister. He was propelled awake, sweating and out of breath.

The next morning, Joamie drove his ATV behind the others, carefully scanning the ground for tracks. He hoped for a caribou or muskox; either would have enough meat to last a while. After a morning of travel, the group was hours from the village. Joamie's eyes scanned the flat landscape continuously, looking for anything that appeared unusual.

It was nearing two a.m. when they finally stopped to set up

camp. Normally, Joamie had no difficulty sleeping in the sunlight, but this time, for some reason, he felt an uneasiness he couldn't shake. While the others slept soundly in tents, Joamie walked away from camp, looking for a spot to relieve himself. He noticed something in the distance. At first, he thought it was a burned-down cabin, but as he got closer his blood ran cold.

It was a door. The door. It looked the same as it had in the winter: standing alone, unfixed to the landscape. He considered waking the other men, but something compelled him toward it. He didn't want to do it, but it was as though he was not in control of his own body. He found himself approaching, despite the feeling that something was very wrong. There was something sinister about the door. The urge to open it was stronger this time. He put his hand on the knob. He remembered his grandmother's warning. He pictured her face as he tried to keep his hand off the knob. It was as though an invisible force had taken over Joamie. A deep breath, and he opened the door. He couldn't help it.

He closed his eyes, half expecting something awful to jump out and eat him. Slowly opening his eyes, he stared through the empty door frame to see the same landscape on the other side. Nothing horrible, no monsters, no demons. He walked back to camp, and, looking over his shoulder, saw that the door had quietly vanished.

Joamie felt unsettled. He told himself he should feel relieved, but something nagged at him. Deep down he knew that couldn't be it. He felt as though the door wasn't finished with him. The anticipation of what lay ahead was nerve-racking. He did his best to shove his concern aside and act like everything was fine.

Three days later, the group arrived back in the village on schedule. The hunting party had killed two large bison, enough meat to last a few weeks. Joamie found his grandmother in the kitchen when he arrived home. She was sitting with her Bible in front of her. Reading glasses hung from a string around her neck. She visibly shivered when he walked in.

"We were successful," he said, smiling as he placed cuts of meat inside the freezer. Ethel sat stone-faced.

"Aren't you happy? You can make stew tonight," he said.

"Go into the backyard," she said.

He opened the back door. A raven was lying right at his feet, almost as though it were waiting for him, horribly injured. Its neck was broken, and blood pooled around its body. Joamie bent down to get a closer look. He then noticed the yard was littered with at least a dozen dead birds, all bloody and broken. Joamie recoiled in horror. He stepped quickly back inside the house.

"You opened the door," Ethel said, her tone filled with disappointment and fear. Her words pained her grandson. Joamie, wide-eyed, was speechless. He lowered his head. He searched for something to say.

"I . . . I'm sorry," he muttered.

"I'm afraid it's too late for sorry."

A blood-curdling howl came from outside. It was almost animalistic; it was so deep and unnatural. Darrell was outside, blood flowing from his eyes. His piercing screams brought out half the village. Most people just stood around watching, shocked at the sight. A few ran to Darrell's side in an attempt to help. He writhed and flailed so violently that no one was able to hold onto him. Blood spurted from his face, spraying those closest to him. Joamie stood watching from the window. He wanted to help his friend but found himself frozen in fear.

"There is nothing we can do," Ethel said. She put down the Bible and motioned for Joamie to join her at the table.

"When I was a girl, my mother told me about something that happened when she was a child. Her uncle claimed a door had appeared before him. He had been using sled dogs to cross from his hunting grounds back to his camp. There was a blizzard. His dogs became agitated. He saw a door, standing on its own. He felt the evil that lay behind it, but he couldn't help himself. He had to open it. Nobody believed him, of course. They laughed at him, said he must be sick in the head to come up with such a crazy story."

Ethel paused. She began to cry but stifled her tears with a tissue. "Then people began to die. First, they suffered in an unspeakable manner."

Joamie thought of Darrell, lying right outside on the gravel road, writhing and contorting in pain.

"The sickness spread, and everyone in the camp was dead in a few days," Ethel said. "Aside from my mother and her older brother, who fled early on. For some strange reason, their lives were spared."

The pair sat in silence for a moment. Screams could be heard outside.

"We can leave," he said to his grandmother.

"And go where?"

"We can take the ATV to Coral Inlet. The weather is good, endless daylight. We can make it."

Ethel didn't respond.

"We can make it, Grandma. Grandma!"

Ethel sat quietly, picking her Bible back up and continuing to read. She was so calm that it made Joamie feel panicky. He got up abruptly from the table and began to pack. He shoved some clothes, food, and a few other necessities in a duffle bag. He went back to the kitchen to tell Ethel it was time to leave, but just as he reached the doorway, he felt something wet on his face. Joamie touched his eyes, which had begun to sting. He looked at his hand to see blood.

Ethel looked up at him as tears of blood fell onto the pages of her Bible.

"God help us," she said.

Wheetago War II: Summoners

Richard Van Camp

YOU KNOW WHAT HAPPENED AT BEAR HOUSE. THREE WEEKS
ago . . .

For the record, I cannot hear most of what you're saying. I've
lost most of my hearing in both ears so I'm just going to start.

No, Sir. I cannot answer that. That is our Clan Business and you
know better. You released the names of those who passed before
you should have. There's a fourth sister and this is how she finds
out? After Kateri's through with me, she'll come looking for you. I
promise. We have protocol for a reason and you blew it. Can I start?

Okay, I think we can all agree that what happened to us out at
The Halfway led to the taking of Outpost 5.

For those of you who don't know . . . we had a bush school
on a field trip outside of Outpost 5. This was at what we called
The Halfway. You could either come with us and Teacher Norma to
get porcupine quills or you could set snares for rabbits and grouse
with Yellow Hand at The Gate. The children we were charged with
were the group that chose Norma, Yellow Hand's wife. She was

with their daughter, Sarah, and seven other smaller kids. Each was marked in the way of the walrus or the caribou: this signified if they were guardians of the land or the sea. Each child and teacher had Silencers around their chests with life jackets that were brightly lit so they were hard to lose in case there needed to be a quick evacuation or body Recon.

I remember Norma. Her fierce eyes. How she sang. No song or prayer will ever be whole now without her. I mean that.

"Okay, everyone. Gather round," she said. "Today we're going to learn how to harvest porcupine quills."

I remember that Sarah, her daughter, asked: "Mom, is this the trail where the *Na acho* used to pass?"

Norma nodded: "Yes, my girl. A long time ago, there were Na acho, the giant ones. They used to pass here. See that mountain? Look along the sides. That was all scraped smooth by giant beavers as they made their way south for war."

We, the kids and the guards who were supposed to be guarding them all, looked up in astonishment. You could see the huge smooth scrape against the face of it. The Na acho were the ancient ones, the giants that used to roam the earth: giant beavers, giant eagles. Christ, we could sure use them now.

"Will they ever return?" a girl asked.

"Of course they will," Sarah said. "With great evil spilling into the world . . . we have to have faith."

The group quieted at this. We were all amazed someone so young could be so wise. She had been spending time with Old Man, the Chanter. I wondered if those were her words or his.

"Dove said they heard mermaids singing under the ice here last spring," one of the quieter boys said. Amos was his name.

Stephen said: "My mom said Dove is both a girl and a boy."

Who is Dove? Dove's our Shifter. Our Moon Watcher. Yes, Dove is a Shifter. You tell me what he or she or they is or are. I'll tell you what: after you hear what happened you won't be rolling your eyes when I mention that name. Can I continue?

Okay, so Norma held her hands out. "Oh now," she said. "Let's focus on the lesson of today."

She then motioned for us all to approach the body of a dead porcupine as she pulled on thick gloves. "Okay, so here we are. I saw this little one yesterday when we were picking berries. We drop tobacco in honour of this little life's passing."

As I scanned the horizon and trees, I could smell the fresh, smoky tobacco. The students knew not to distract us as they passed a pouch around. There were four other guards. I remember that. Kateri's three sisters and a distant man—"Stanley," they called him—who could drop a Wheetago from a mile away. Stanley was an ace at using his .30-30 to take out the eyes of a Shovel Head. I seen that myself at least five times.

What happens when they're blinded? The others eat 'em. It's pretty: to see Hair Eaters turn on each other like that.

So the teachers and students dropped tobacco and offered it to the earth and to our Mother.

"Today," Norma said, "we give thanks for all we have. My husband's birthday is soon approaching, and I want to make him new moccasins. Our camp is low on beads, but you can use porcupine quills to decorate just about anything if you know what to do. Lucky for all of you, Aunty knows what to do."

The kids giggled and beamed. I could feel it. No matter what happened after, I can go back to that last exact perfect moment.

Uncle Ned was with us. To this day, I'm not sure why he was there. Bored, maybe. Maybe he wanted to feel the sun on his face. Maybe he wanted to watch the children learn. We'll never know now, will we?

The guards: each was tattooed, pierced, and marked with the sign of the caribou. Two had dreadlocks and a side shave. One had her hair tied tightly in a bun. Again, each one of us had military grade Silencers. All it takes is one Wheetago to scream and it can freeze the lot of you. I seen that . . . or I should say I seen what a group of humans looks like after. You'll never forget it. The Wheetago suck the brains out of their victims through their eyes after they're frozen. That means you see your killer coming. You can't do a thing.

We were all armed with long spears, flares, handguns, rifles. I'd left my long spear at home that day, thinking I had a rifle and a side piece and a flare gun. Stupid. Stupid. Stupid. Stupid.

It was a beautiful day. The leaves were yellow, gold. Frost had been on the grass just that morning. No wind. You could hear for miles.

I thought I saw movement out of the corner of my eye. My hunting glasses. If a bird passes, it catches the reflection. When I'm hyper aware, I move quick. We all turned. Nothing. Can we come back to this later? Why? Cuz I have a theory, that's why.

Okay . . .

Norma showed her daughter and the students to take care in pulling out the porcupine quills with a tool she'd built. They were pliers she'd modified. I took time to admire the shawls that Norma and her daughter wore. Norma's shawl covered her belly and had a caribou on it. Sarah's had a caribou as well, but it was a young one. Innocent. The women, they had started loomin' and what they were turning out was beautiful. It brought hope, which is a dangerous but welcome thing. We were all feeling human again. Norma was pregnant, eight months. And here she was with her daughter preparing gifts for Yellow Hand's birthday. I thought to make him one of my famous T knives. They're small but lethal.

On this expedition, Sarah was the oldest. I can only truly say I knew three of the smaller ones. I'm proud of that. The Outpost was growing. Again, we had hope. Strength in numbers. My little buddies were Tyler the Blond, Alex the Bulldog, and Shane the Fearless. Those were my names for them.

I remember a snicker. Uncle Ned was smiling. He looked young; his face was clear, radiant. He looked at the twin suns before he met my eyes, and I admired his braids, how his wife had braided stained moosehide into them. He always carried his Silencers around his throat. All he'd need to do is duck and they'd be on in a heartbeat. I'd copied him the second I'd noticed the way he had shaved them down and covered them with moose—

Ned winced. I remember watching him as he winced. There was a twitch to his face. That was when it happened. He winced when one of the guards—Old Mah—the way she looked at a bird on the ground with its wings fanned out. It was a magpie. Old Mah was still wearing her teddy bear in a baby carrier. She lost her baby. You know the Wheetago. One of their priests—or Oracles, as you call them—sewed what was left of her boy into the bark of a tree—

Sorry.

Okay, the bird was face down to the earth—alive—with its wings fanned out. *It's eating something*, I thought. I remember that. We looked farther. I drew my gun. There were six other birds like this. Face down. Wings out. Raking their beaks into the earth to eat something.

Old Mah asked, "What is it?"

Ned quipped, "Even the birds are praying now."

One of the birds looked at all of us. A calligraphy of light—pure blue fire—erupted from between its eyes as it turned in the air and spun.

What we had witnessed was over and something cold flashed through me.

All seven birds then exploded into flight.

We realized something together and Uncle Ned shouted, "We need to leave this place—NOW!"

I looked to our group: Norma, wearing special gloves, was lifting the porcupine. She was pulling a quill out. Sarah was beside her, holding out a bag for her mom.

It sprang back to life. The porcupine detonated back to life in her hands. It wasn't dead at all. Or maybe it was, but it was a spell. A trap.

Its eyes. They looked like eggs boiled to death.

The porcupine grabbed Norma's ears and immediately tore her face apart in front of all of us.

She and Ned screamed at the same time: "No!!"

Norma yelled, "Oh God. Oh God. Oh God—shoot it. Save the children. Shoot it! Sarah!!"

As I hit my safety and raised my rifle, I saw the faces of the guards and the children: pure horror.

The porcupine hissed at all of us with pure hatred before tearing back into Norma's eye.

I heard a click from Uncle's gun behind me. Then another. And another. Ned pushed me and yelled, "Shoot it!" But I couldn't.

Norma's shawl flew. Her belly. The baby. I couldn't locate the target with all the hair and blood that was flying. I could not hit Sarah who was trying to help or that baby inside Norma. *Save the baby*, I kept thinking. *Save Sarah and the baby. I'm sorry, Yellow Hand. It's too late for your wife.*

"Save the children!" someone yelled. "Back to the Outpost!"

"Norma, you fight it," Uncle Ned yelled with a measured voice as he drew his backup rifle. "Think of Sarah and your little one on the way. Fight it so Sarah can run to us. Somebody, shoot that creature! My gun's jammed!"

The porcupine hissed again and tore through Norma's cheek. Blood streamed down her arms, her neck. It was a blur of ripping, quills, tearing. Her hair flew. Chunks of it.

Norma's spine then snapped as she bent completely in half backwards. The Wheetago spirit had her.

Ned pushed me again. "Shoot it, goddamned you. She's Wheetago. Kill her and that thing before it gets all of us." I looked and his pistol was by his feet. He'd tossed it after it wouldn't fire. His rifle was drawn but it dry fired and he tossed that, too.

One of the guards yelled, "Get the kids!! RUN!!"

The problem with kids is that—as many drills as we ran with them—they all ran off in different directions. Who can blame them? We were all scared. I remember the safety going off on my gun as I aimed to fire. I heard Sarah call, "Mom?"

Click—

My gun jammed.

Click—

I kept pulling my trigger. What should have been two skull shots were nothing.

Ned yelled, "Sarah, run to me right now. Come!"

Sarah bolted towards him. "Uncle!"

I dropped my rifle and pulled out my pistol. *Click—*

Again. Nothing was working. None of our guns were firing. We were all pulling our triggers for nothing.

Norma shot back upright but crooked, looking at all of us, but it wasn't her. She had turned Wheetago. Her eyes were pure hate and the way she started advancing toward us, all hunched up, taking a huge breath. . . .

"Shit," I yelled. "Do not let her yell. Shoot her!" I kept waiting for someone to shoot her, but we were all frozen in fear. She was pregnant. None of our guns worked. Not even my pistol. I dropped it, ducked into my Silencers and pulled out my flare gun. I remembered to aim for her mouth before she started biting us or letting out one of their Hell cries.

But she did the strangest thing. Norma looked to the sharpest rock jutting upwards and then started slamming her face over and over on it, splitting her jaw in half, breaking her teeth into a maw of fangs.

"Silencers!" I yelled. "Do not let her scream. Who has the children?"

"Got 'em!" one of the sisters yelled.

"Get them back to the Outpost and send help!" I yelled.

"Done!"

I assumed they left. I found out later they couldn't.

Sarah had run toward us but spun around to run back toward her mom. "Mom!?"

Ned yelled again, "Sarah, run to me! Put on your goddamned Silencers. Stay away from your mother. She's not her anymore."

The porcupine and Norma saw Sarah run toward them, thinking she could maybe save the baby somehow. We never saw someone Turn with a baby still inside them. Norma's face was now that of a bleeding skull watching her own daughter, and I could tell she was getting ready to bite. The porcupine lunged.

All I heard was Ned dry firing his backup pistol at both of them, but we kept hearing *"click—clicks"* from both of us. From all of us, actually.

Somebody yelled. It wasn't a command. It was a yell of fear. I looked and three of the guards were under attack. What had them had come from above. I seen a rope of guts spray out from one of the sisters. Aggie, her name was. That rope was as long as her braids. This Wheetago looked like a new kind: a Reaper, they call it. With the beak.

The porcupine then lunged toward Uncle Ned and me. The porcupine was midair when an arrow nailed its head to a tree. This had been fired by Dove, the Shifter, who was returning with two jugs of fresh water.

No one was more surprised than Dove, who was not wearing their Silencers. They were still around their throat. I remember that.

Dove managed to say "Oh God" when Norma started to charge toward Dove. Norma was starving. She started to scream.

Ned yelled, "COVER!!"

Dove says that "by luck" they flipped their rapier and caught Norma perfectly by the throat. She was impaled but "alive." She was immobilized for now and clawing the air. She could not scream.

The way Dove caught her was amazing.

I pulled my machete out and made my way toward Norma. This had to be quick.

Dove reloaded their spear gun.

And that was when we were hit with the grenade.

It tore Ned in half and knocked me out. Dove, too.

I must have been out for a good five minutes because when I woke up, I was covered in what was left of Ned. The sisters and Stanley were eaten in half. Splitters had gotten to them. They'd been skinned and gutted. Splitters? If you don't know . . . they step on your arms and pull you in half. It's a horrible thing to witness. All Wheetago choke on moose fat. We've yet to see if this works on Splitters. Oracles? Yes. We've seen them gag on it and drop. So far, none resurrect themselves. The children were all gone. Even the baby. They'd taken the . . . let's just say they'd taken all of the children and the one that was wanting to be born. They were all gone.

Sorry?

Oh. My theory. Let me think about this: they say that Earth had seven billion humans before the Wheetago returned, right? I think that was their magic number. I think they warmed the world and unthawed themselves from whatever Hell they came from. I think seven billion was the magic number for the food they'd need to make the world maggoty with them and their kind.

Maybe they Turned God, too. Who knows?

Sure. Fuck. I could eat a bullet. Millions have. But I think of this as a game now. Something's happening. Something bigger than all of us. Even them.

It's an awakening.

I think if I make it, I'm gonna witness an answer to all our prayers.

Are four horsemen gonna come racing across the sky?

Are we gonna hear the trumpets over their screams?

Or was the world always theirs?

Have we been praying to the wrong God all this time?

As sure as something made all of us, I kinda want to see what's gonna happen next because who do they worship? Do you ever think of that? When they're standing there swaying together under the moon. Like stalks of wheat. Who are they praying to?

What? No. I don't think this was ever our world. We were just fattening it up for them.

What's that? Yes. Well, that's why I'm here.

It was a trap. All of it. That's how they got the Outpost. We had hydroponics, medicines, water filtration systems, heating, housing for everyone, showers. Gardens and hothouses for miles. Everyone had duties: fishing, hunting, cleaning, fire, patrols, training, schools.

I think with all our scouts and traps, they knew it would take one hell of a toll on their numbers just to charge, so they put a spell on that porcupine to trick us. I also know that the Wheetago can freeze guns. It's happened before but not in the numbers that happened to us. Their power is growing. They're problem solving and they can sense electricity. Everyone has to use spear guns now. It's mandatory to bring your rapiers. The scouts seem to remember trails, but if they're using their magic, what do we have? We have Old Man and his wife. We have Dove. No, I do not know what Dove is, but I am here to nominate them for the Mark of the Butterfly. You bet your ass, I am. Dove goddamned saved me. I pray he and she wakes up soon.

Yes, it's a coma, but we are all hopeful.

Okay, you think on that. Dove's marked already. They won't be forgetting Dove. You know they remember faces, right? And you know the Wheetago are a praying people. Folks have reported them whispering to the moon. Thousands of them standing there, just praying. Who are they praying to?

And why do they want our children? You ever think of that? It ain't killing. It's something more. Something . . . for their rituals. We seen their altars out there on the land. Some of our scouts have seen them smudging with human hair. Are they calling something through us? What if there is something bigger coming? What if these are just the scouts?

I have had a lot of time to think about this, and I only seen three kinds of them. I have talked to refugees that saw one that could fly. I have seen Shovel Heads. They're slow but they ain't stupid, and it takes a lot of stabbing to take one of them down, never mind a herd of them, but the standard drone, yeah, who hasn't. But an Oracle. One of their wizards? No. We heard reports of the flames above them when they walk. I seen that fire over the porcupine's head and the magpie's head. I still don't know what to think of that.

But what if they want children . . . to have them . . . like . . . to make them. We have reports of folks who saw the Mother birthing them from her mouth. That's law. That's how they're made. Unless you're bit. Then it's all over. You're Turned.

But one of them kids: Shane. He was my godson. I have to walk by his grandmother every day, and I would have gladly given my life for his, but when there are no bodies there's no peace.

So where are they?

Where are those kids?

What if they want children? What if what's left of them as human remembers having children? We must never let them cross.

Because what if they're raising them as their own? If so, what are they raising them for?

I sit here before you to say that I will happily lead anyone back to the Outpost. You need a scout? I'm your man. We need everything there to maintain all we have left.

Because we have to take back our kingdom. But, first things first, we have to find our children.

You have my word. Yes, Sir.

That's a good question: that grenade. It could have been thrown by a human working for the Wheetago. Yes, I've heard of the farms in the South. I can't think of anyone in our camp who had something like that. It also hit me that what got the sisters came from either the trees or the earth. Either way, we lost a lot of friends who were also incredible soldiers. I am going to repeat: they were skinned and gutted. I know that isn't new, but where were my Silencers and where were the Silencers of Uncle Ned and Dove? They were gone when we woke up. Also, some of our magazines. The Wheetago don't use our weapons. I don't think they know how. But if it was humans helping them—what if they—the human helpers—what if they are biding their time to kill whoever's keeping 'em hostage?

And I have news: I recognized Shane's arm band on the grass beside me when I woke up. I was there when it was given to him in ceremony and I carry it with me now. I took it to Old Man. He prayed on it. He said Shane's still alive, and I believe it. I gave Shane a knife just that morning. It's one I made. I have to believe that boy is alive. I need to believe it. I swear . . . when I get to Heaven, I'm gonna kill God and all his angels for what they didn't do down here when we needed them most. I'll tell you what. Hell would be kinder than what we had to face. Earth ain't ours anymore. I could feel it every day after the Three Day War. That's all it took: three days to claim a God and a planet?

Maybe we had it coming.

But with what time I got left on this planet, I'm gonna use it to go get those kids back for their families . . . for our family. Count me in. As for the mother of them all, I cannot wait to kill her.

Yes, Sir. Thank you for listening. *Mahsi cho.*

Oh. Before I forget: we never found that porcupine. I have every reason to believe it's still out there.

Mahsi.

Revenge
Thomas Anguti Johnston

A MAN IS ALONE AT THE FLOE EDGE. SPRING HAS JUST BEGUN TO lengthen the days. The sky is clear and the sun shines, but it is still cold and the ice is still solid. The water gently laps against the ice edge and a mature ringed seal pokes its head up to take in the weather. The man who is alone quietly chambers a bullet into his rifle and takes aim with steady breaths. The first of the seagulls has arrived and as it squawks the ringed seal looks up. The lone man pulls the trigger.

The lone man paddles his little floe-edge boat and hooks the seal with his *niksik*, pulling it back to the ice. Once he has hauled the seal atop the ice, along with the boat, he takes a deep breath. He exhales slowly and chants, "Come to me and feed on my bounty. Come and I will give you more."

The lone man takes one last deep breath, starts his snowmobile. Leaving behind the seal he shot.

The man who was alone at the floe edge is now parking his snowmobile in the shelter of a bay. He lives alone, on the mainland, by the coast. His home is a cabin facing south sheltered by a low hill. In the spring he lives off the ocean creatures and the birds migrating north to nest and fatten.

The man prepares a meal and thinks of Siqiniq, the woman who once lived here with him. Once the silence would be filled with chatter as she cooked or sewed clothing. But she has been gone for many years now.

"I was unlucky again, only seeing one seal that sank before I could retrieve it," the man imagines telling the woman. He can't even imagine telling her the truth. *I've been leaving dead animals at the floe edge and purposely sinking catches for years.*

"I know you will do the best you can for us," the lone man imagines the woman saying.

"Still, it would have been nice. . . ." The man's voice trails off.

"9-3-4, *tavvaniippit?* 9-3-4, are you there? 4-5-3." The CB radio crackles loudly.

The lone man picks up the speaking piece of the radio and holds it up to his mouth. 934 is not his call sign but it has been so long since he talked to anyone. After Siqiniq left he would speak with her over CB, but the last time was five years ago, when she said she'd only ever talk to him in person. She was encouraging him to return home with her.

"*Tavva* 9-3-4, 9-3-4 here. How are you 4-5-3?" another CB user replies.

The lone man puts down the speaking piece and shuts off the CB. He turns to his food and slowly consumes the last of his jarred pickles. He pushes Siqiniq out of his mind and focuses on his plans.

It won't be long now, he thinks to himself. *The last of the bait is nearly set. It's because of them I am alone. It's because of them I only feel pain and loneliness.*

The next morning, the lone man watches the sun rise out his window while he finishes up a small breakfast. He ponders if his parents had survived if he would find the scene to be picturesque. With a huff the lone man begins to dress for the day. Once the sun is high enough above the horizon, he climbs the low hill. Near the top is a boulder, and hidden beneath it is an old box made of carved driftwood. The lone man went to great lengths in the Far North to acquire this box and its content. The lone man takes the box back to the cabin, where he opens it. Inside is a carefully wrapped knife in cloth, its age unknowable to the eye.

The blade in the cloth is sharpened and engraved red walrus tusk, the blood-red ivory of one of the giant carnivorous walruses that live far, far to the west and prey on seals and smaller walruses. The blade carries depictions of animals larger than ones living today. Great birds near the top of the blade, then whales, caribou, wolves, walruses, and at the base of the blade is the *nanurluk*, the king of bears. The depictions almost seem to move. An ancient tool, much more than an ornate knife. The lone man cannot hold it for long out of fear. Carefully, he wraps it once again in the cloth and returns it to the carved driftwood box. Instead of placing it beneath the boulder, the lone man packs it, with his rifle and bullets, in his *savikkuvik*, the box that holds his gear on his *qamutiik*.

The lone man is once again at the floe edge, where he left the mature seal carcass the day before. All that is left of the kill is blood-stained snow. The lone man doesn't wait long before a young ringed seal pops its head out of the water. With a breath, practised movement, and unnatural ease, the lone man shoots the seal and brain matter splashes onto the water beyond its head. The lone man doesn't bother putting his floe-edge boat into the water this time. He watches the seal body bob around and slowly sink. Sink like an upturned *qajaq*.

With a grin, the lone man unpacks his thermos and pours hot water into a cup. He drops an orange pekoe tea bag into the cup and liberates a biscuit from a cardboard container. The lone man watches sea birds fly in their fast, snakelike pattern, feet above the open water. He recalls his childhood while the crunching of the biscuits in his mouth is slowly overtaken by a faint beating coming from somewhere far below.

Many years ago the lone man was but a boy living in a settlement in the High Arctic. He was kind, and his parents loved him very much. In those days, everything seemed to glow and all was vibrant. That all stopped when all the boats went out for whale hunting one fall morning. The wind had picked up and the waves crashed hard onto the beach. No boats that had left that morning returned that night; no boats returned until the next day. One by one the boats appeared, but not the boy's parents' boat, a sturdy freighter canoe. Most who arrived that day couldn't look the boy in the eye, perhaps ashamed or afraid. All the boy could get out of those who returned was a frantic gaze or some nonsense about never returning to that place. His parents' boat had sunk with them on board.

The orphan boy had only one friend. Siqiniq. She was the only one who would stand up for him, who would protect him from torturers. Since his parents' boat sank to the bottom of the sea, the orphan often was mistreated by members of the community. The orphan boy quickly developed an unhealthy attachment to Siqiniq. What he thought was love, or maybe a version of love that doesn't know what it is until it is too late.

He was often bullied, and one day the bullying escalated. Another boy knocked Siqiniq down in front of him, and the boy— who was more of a man by this time—flew into a rage. The orphan's vision turned to red. When he came to his senses, Siqiniq was pulling him away, saying that she thought the bully might be dead.

The two, the orphan boy and Siqiniq, ran away. They stole Siqiniq's family's snowmobile and whatever gear they could find and they fled. The orphan boy could only think of one place they could go. To the area where his parents had died.

The last, biscuity sip of the lone man's tea goes down cold. His smile has been replaced with an intense stare. The lone man shakes the last drops of his tea out of his cup and onto the snow, then packs the cup away. He pauses a moment and becomes still and silent. The sea birds are quiet and the sound of the waves lapping against the ice is muffled, as if his ears are stuffed with cotton. The blue sky has greyed, but there is not a cloud in sight. A deep, low rumbling rises from the ocean in drum beats. No, heartbeats. The waves have stopped completely now, and the water is still except for ripples coinciding with the heartbeats. All colour drains away from the world. The lone man is no longer in the world he inhabited a moment ago.

The lone man moves swiftly toward the carved driftwood box and picks it up. He walks to the snowmobile, where he left his rifle, the clip loaded but without a bullet in the chamber. He sets the box on the raised end of the snowmobile seat and grabs his rifle, flicking the safety off and half cocking it before returning his attention to the box. As the lone man works it open and unwraps the walrus-tusk knife, he takes long, deep breaths. He does this all with his eyes closed. He listens to every sound. The world is dominated by the sea's heartbeat. The beat doesn't seem to be getting any louder, but there is a second sound. The rubbery crunch of soft snow being trudged upon. Slow at first. But the footfalls grow closer and closer until they sound as if a four-legged creature is running towards the lone man. He finally opens his eyes. The curved walrus-tusk blade in his hand is a slash of bright red across the grey landscape.

The lone man tucks the tusk knife into his belt, pointing his head towards the approaching animal. The largest polar bear he has ever seen is charging straight at him, as low as a giant bear could be to the ice. The heartbeat continues but now the footsteps are louder, along with the puffs of the giant bear. The lone man cocks a round into the chamber of his rifle and takes aim at the approaching bear. It is still twenty yards away but speedily subtracting yards with each step. Fifteen yards, ten yards, five yards, and the bear rears up with a roar. The blast from the roar shakes the chest of the lone man. The bear stands fourteen feet tall, towering over the lone man. The rifle barks back and a red mark appears where the giant bear's heart is. The bear coughs blood as it falls forward to all fours, but it still has the strength to make another charge. The lone man suspected this moment would come to pass and is prepared for exactly this instant.

The lone man drops his gun and reaches for his belt. He pulls out the knife with the blade up. The bear lunges one more time at the man, clearing the snowmobile easily. The lone man spins low, away from the giant teeth, and stabs at the neck of the bear. Dark red liquid arcs across the colourless sky and snow. The bear huffs and moves slowly to a seated position. The giant bear huffs again, shakes its head in confusion, and lowers into a crouching position, readying itself for a final lunge. The lone man bolts for the qamutiik and turns as the bear leaps impossibly far toward the man and the qamutiik. The lone man was hoping for another second to prepare for the strike and has to adjust his movement. He turns to avoid the mouth aimed at his neck, stabbing at the animal's underarm, which is exposed as the bear swipes a paw midair. The man's arm is slashed and bloodied as they twist in midair, but he manages to drive the blade of the red walrus tusk to the hilt and into the heart of the giant bear. Air leaves the giant bear's lungs in bloody coughs. The lone man holds the knife in the giant bear until he feels the last breath escape its mouth.

The giant bear now lies where it landed, on the qamutiik. The lone man withdraws the blade from the heart of the beast, wipes most of the blood in the snow, and returns the blade to his belt. He knows he only has a short time. Satisfied with how the bear lies on the qamutiik, the lone man stumbles toward the snowmobile, his arm throbbing as blood leaves his body through three large gashes that slice through his outerwear and into his meat to the bone. With only the use of his right arm, he straps the gun over his shoulder and pulls at the ignition cord of his vehicle. He can't pull very hard and the machine doesn't come to life. The lone man takes a breath to push his panic away. The heartbeat of the sea has quickened. *Is it louder? Is it closer?*

He steadies himself and pulls the cord once more. The machine putters and dies again. *Damn.* He should have left it running. *Sloppy.* The low rumble of the ocean heartbeat shakes everything now. The knife in his belt vibrates harder and harder with each beat. The top layer of snow dances upon the ice. The lone man pulls the cord again.

The snowmobile comes to life. The lone man jumps onto the seat and revs the engine. It strains against the weight of the qamutiik and the giant bear. Slowly, the snowmobile picks up speed. The heartbeat seems to surround the lone man now, and the ice begins to warp beneath him. He struggles to keep control with only one usable arm, but he makes his way away from the floe edge. He fears looking back, but does. An impossibly large polar bear paw emerges from the water and onto the edge where he slew the bear only moments before. The man's knife stirs, and the blade digs into his thigh. A second paw and a gigantic snout appear. Although the lone man's snowmobile is straining and the engine is whining audibly, the only sound to be heard is the heartbeat—and now the bear's breath. The gigantic bear pulls itself onto the ice and is now on all fours. The nanurluk. The legendary king of all bears, the fiercest predator. From forepaw to ears, it stands twenty feet high, easily fifty if it stood on its hind legs. The quick action of the lone man has given him a head start, and with the momentum he has accumulated, he travels fast upon the ice.

At first he drives toward his camp but thanks to another stab into his thigh from the walrus blade, he recalls his intent. He turns away from the mainland and toward an island, far off on the horizon. He struggles to keep speed, but he dares not slow even a fraction. Behind him he can hear the nanurluk take its first strides in pursuit. Each step sends waves through the thick ice, which the lone man uses to his advantage, riding them toward the island. The island where he was born. Where he lost his parents. Where he paralyzed a young man and was banished. The place where he was treated so poorly. The concentration of all his hate. . . .

***

The nanurluk, being an ancient creature of the sea, needs to reacquaint its legs with being above the water. Angrily the nanurluk stumbles about like a calf learning to walk. The dot of the lone man disappearing ahead of him. The bear lets out a great roar, loud enough to be heard by all Inuit in the Arctic. Bit by bit, the nanurluk finds his feet and rhythm. The bear chases its fallen mate, the dead bear being pulled away by the snowmobile, the one the human has killed. The human has a familiar stench. *Vermin, how dare it*, the nanurluk thinks as it watches the mate slayer drive away.

The snowmobile seems to be driving toward an island long inhabited by Inuit. The nanurluk figures it can catch up before they arrive. But before the nanurluk gets any closer, the mate slayer cuts loose the qamutiik and the giantess bear that lies lifeless upon it. The nanurluk overcomes the qamutiik and sniffs at the carcass. With one lick, it turns over the fourteen-foot giant. Death is what it tastes. Death and an old, familiar taste. The taste of the only blade that has ever pierced the nanurluk's thick hide. The nanurluk lets out another shockwave of a roar and resumes pursuit of the mate slayer.

***

The lone man knew he would have to cut the qamutiik loose before he reached the island. The nanurluk is faster than he could have imagined. He figures he is close enough, though, and the beast will continue pursuing him. As if to confirm this suspicion the nanurluk lets out a sorrowful and angry roar behind him. He can now drive at full speed, zipping over the ice. The walrus blade shakes hard, as if it has its own life, but it doesn't shake free of his belt. The lone man makes it to the settlement on the island. The first thing he sees Siqiniq's childhood house.

How could I forget? thinks the lone man. *How I have been so blind?*

Siqiniq left the lone man all those years ago when she learned she was pregnant. She had been talking to people from the settlement about the incident that had left the bully paralyzed, not dead like they thought. She had tried convincing the lone man to return to the settlement with her, where she had family. But he refused. The lone man—so focused on his anger, his pain, his revenge—forgot that Siqiniq would be here . . . and not just her . . . he had to hurry.

Panic overtakes him. The giantess bear, who slashed his arm open, didn't invoke this much panic in him. The legendary nanurluk didn't strike panic in him, either. It was all part of his plan. No, his only panic is from remembering the one person alive who ever treated him with kindness—and that she is in the settlement he has just set the nanurluk upon. He must find her before it is too late.

The nanurluk approaches the settlement as night begins to fall. The dog teams tied up at the edge of town make as much racket as they can. *Dogs. Cur-scum*, thinks the nanurluk. *They bark but they are puny, like lemmings.* With a flick of a paw one team is knocked dead. The nanurluk will destroy the entire settlement to find the one responsible for the death of his mate. Wood and aluminum roofs stand no chance against the giant bear. It moves toward the edge of town, careful to sniff for the smell of the mate slayer and its red-tusk weapon. Some inhabitants fire their guns, but it is no use. The bullets only bounce off the hide of the nanurluk.

"Siqiniq!" calls the lone man. "Siqiniq! Where are you!?" The nanurluk is now at the edge of town. The pops of the community's guns can be heard, but the dog teams are now silent. People scream and run. There is only one place to flee to. Only one place to hide. At the far end of the settlement on the island there is a range of cliffs with deep cuts and caves carved into it. Already the lone man can see people scrambling up the least steep parts of the cliff base. *It will be there that I will find Siqiniq*, the lone man thinks. He drives through the streets in the direction of the cliff.

The nanurluk rips another roof off a house. Inside he sees a man restricted to a bed. The man seems to not be able to use his body, except to scream feebly. His body is lifeless, paralyzed. The nanurluk ends the pain of this person with one stab of a claw. The feeble screams die. The nanurluk abandons the idea of going house by house and lies low, as if stalking prey. The nanurluk closes its eyes and focuses all its senses on the scent of the townspeople. It inhales a great breath. There is a familiar smell that it can pick out in the mess of odours. The smell of the mate slayer, but not quite, similar in many ways. It decides to follow the trail of this scent. The nanurluk stalks forward in a crouch, following its nose.

The lone man drives by many people running for their lives. Many he recognizes from the time before he was banished. Many recognize him, too. Many young ones that he has never seen. He did not realize there would be young ones here. He cannot dwell on the thought. He must find Siqiniq or draw the nanurluk away. He must decide quickly. The lone man is knocked off his machine by another driver panicking to get to the cliff. The lone man is thrown and the walrus blade cuts into his leg. He pulls it out with a painful growl. He tries to apply pressure to the new wound, but his left hand has become useless. He manages to get to his feet nonetheless. He yells for Siqiniq with the blade held out in his hand.

The nanurluk approaches its prey with stealth. From the breathing pattern, he can tell his prey is a boy child. A boy child with the scent of the mate slayer. The boy is with another, a woman, running towards the cliffs. She is trying to help him escape the nanurluk. But the nanurluk has only once lost its prey, and that is now a forgotten memory. The nanurluk slyly closes in on the boy child and the woman, using the houses as cover.

The lone man fights against the tide of people running for the cliffs. He calls for Siqiniq, but no one replies to him. He is now desperate. He must come up with a plan. He has been so consumed with the thought of revenge, of punishing those who treated him worse than an insect, he never acknowledged the faults in his plan, or the safety of the one who truly cared about him. The lone man drew the nanurluk to this settlement where he only recognizes half the people, the other half having never done him any harm. So they could die in the jaws of the beast. The lone man asks himself if this is what revenge is. *Losing everything good and being alone? No, this can't be.* He must be able to stop this before she is taken by the nanurluk.

The lone man raises the blood-red walrus-tusk blade of old and yells with all his might.

The nanurluk can smell the boy and the woman just beyond the next building. The nanurluk creeps silently up the side and strains to glimpse its prey through the darkening night. There they are, running as fast as the boy child can toward the cliffs. The nanurluk pounces for the boy and the woman, but they turn to observe the source of the man's shriek.

Siqiniq is trying her best to get her son to the safety of the cliffs. A monster has descended upon her community and many will be lost, but if only she can get to the—a familiar voice bellows out from some-where to her right. She turns to look, and her son stumbles forward onto his belly. She sees him and suddenly understands. *The poor lone man* is her last thought before a swift set of jaws scoop her up.

The nanurluk has to adjust slightly in midair to his prey's move-ment. The nanurluk has only the woman in his jaws. Not too far off, the nanurluk hears power in a man's scream. Power drawn from the walrus-tusk blade. The nanurluk realizes it has the wrong prey, but it is too late. The woman with the boy who had the mate slayer's scent is dead. His sharp incisors have pierced her body. Mate for mate.

***

The lone man can see the nanurluk leaping through the air like a predator going in for the kill. A moment later the nanurluk stands on its hind legs, taller than the buildings that surround it. The lone man can see a woman's shape dangling in its jaws. It is too late. The lone man limps toward the nanurluk, walrus-tusk blade raised above his head. He charges after it as best he can.

***

The nanurluk looks toward the yelling man and sees the mate slayer charging at him. The blade of power is raised above its head. The nanurluk raises its left paw and swings it at the puny man who charges alone. The paw freezes where it meets the walrus-tusk blade. A great light bursts from the blade and pushes the nanurluk back. The nanurluk regroups and pounces in anger on the tusk-wielding mate slayer. An even greater light—originating from the point of contact between the blade and the nanurluk—blinds all and seems to stop time.

***

I am the man who is alone. That which preyed on boats from time to time took away my mother and father. When my parents were gone, it was many years before I felt any kind of love again. But I was already different by then. A child who grows without love doesn't grow into a peaceful or rational person. It was too late for me. The love that came too late brought up other feelings. Jealousy. Paranoia. Cowardice. Distrust. The plan was already in formulation by then. Attract the thing that killed my parents and have it kill all who I hated. They left me only scraps and had me sleep with their dogs. I have always been stunted by my one and only goal, I now see. But it is too late.

I have lived in these seas longer even than Nuliajuk. I have seen a great many things. The little pieces of meat left by the floe edge or sunk were never of interest to me. A single seal is much too small a morsel to satisfy my hunger. I feed on the largest sea mammals. Baleen whales being the only thing that can satisfy my needs. I lived peacefully, taking only what I needed, never bothering with the humans. That is until they started setting lures and traps. They call to me, once a generation, the ones with the ancient blade. My life stretches back into the earliest times, when the ocean was new and I was but a cub. I have been bested only once, and I will never be again.

So inconvenient, thinks the nanurluk. *This one had the power, but not the will.* Weary from the day's events the beast trudges back towards the floe edge. In its wake is the lone man, body mangled and cold. The blood-red walrus-tusk knife is nowhere to be seen.

Lounge

Sean Qitsualik-Tinsley and Rachel Qitsualik-Tinsley

ONE HOUR AFTER LOUNGE:

Lighting a match. How does one do it? Her good eye is closed. Charlie always taught her that keeping one's eyes shut can adjust them to darkness. How about one eye? She feels the sides of the box, turns it over between her fingers.

She fumbles. The box falls. She isn't sure what material coats the floor. It's warm, because of the heating system underneath, but it's very hard. The box, two matches rattling inside, sounds like an armload of dishes in the quiet room. She remembers that the floor is green, the colour of pines, and has an absurd thought:

Green's noisy.

She mustn't move. She could step on the box. Worse, she could kick it to some far corner. The room is small, only about three by four metres, so finding a little box should be easy. She could go down on hands and knees, grope in the dark. But she might have to go near the bed. She catches a whiff of something like baby powder. She is reminded of what moves over there.

She stays by the door.

She hears crackly, boyish laughter from the hall outside. Troy. His voice never loses its mocking tone. Could he and the others hear the box fall? Possible. Depends on how close to the door they are. They never used to be interested in her. But then, she remembers what Drashtr said: one can't predict what these kind will become.

"Still hiding, Talli?" calls Ian. "Not so high horsy now. Can't you hear the music, sweets?"

Talli is motionless in the dark. Light breaths, like a bird. Over by the bed, there's a low, shifting noise, as of cloth. Bedsheet?

Ambreen gives it a try.

"This isn't about hurting you," she says, voice clinical as ever. "Just being collegial."

"Yeah," says Troy, "and there's ice cream. . . ."

Giggles.

Talli expects them to say something further. Nothing comes. Maybe they're returning to their usual disinterest. She gives it some minutes. When no more sound comes from beyond the door, Talli squats. Envisioning the points of a compass, another Charlie lesson, she paws her way in a methodical, clockwise circle. The first circle, right around her feet, bears no fruit. She widens, begins again. Nothing. She has to straighten, gasping lightly, since the squat is somehow making her dizzy.

In response to her gasp, unintelligible mutters come from the corner of the room. By the bed. Again, that baby powder smell. A chill rides across her face, over her neck. She squats again. This time, her balance is off. Her foot shifts. Her instep knocks against the little matchbox and she can feel it through her sock. So—when it fell, it settled exactly between her feet.

Talli seizes the box, almost crushing it with relief. She stands, leans against the door frame, listens. Nothing. She opens her one good eye, but the room is still mostly dark. So much for Charlie. She sees only barest shapes, a dark hulk next to her: clothes locker. She imagines that she can see the outline of the bed, but isn't sure. Scantest light limns the door frame.

Using both hands, she edges open the matchbox. She hugs the box, moving slowly to pick out a match. No smell. Her uncle coated his matches so carefully. Talli can feel the waxy polymer he used. Closing the box, she moves one thumbnail over the head of the match, working away the "wax."

Side of box, she thinks. *That's how it lights.*

She draws the match along the box's side. She squints at a reddish spark, but then it dies, leaving her blinder than ever.

Too slow. Now she remembers: Correct speed is needed or the match is ruined.

But what if the matches are just too old? Uncle Charlie said they would last forever. But he never expected her to carry them as an adult. For over thirteen years.

Talli strikes again, faster. She blinks against a flare.

And there's light.

Not enough. She has to tilt the match so that it burns more wood and produces extra light. She still reckons she has about thirty seconds before the heat reaches thumb and forefinger. Lucky that Charlie's matches are long burning. That was his talent: thinking of details. The long game was where he blundered.

Left. Right. Floor. Shelves. Tabletop. Talli's amber eyes are everywhere. Her gaze lingers longest on the bed, where she wastes three seconds. It's as she left it, no blanket or pillow. The sky-blue sheet is still wound into a loose ball on the rumpled spread. She now has less than twenty seconds to find a superior light source, or sacrifice the last match.

Talli takes a step toward the toilet, halts.

Corner of her vision. Movement.

The flame flickers, twisting shadows across the room. One of the shadows is new. It's cast by a limb, reaching up from between the bed and wall, moving like a lazy yawn. Almost like a baby's arm, but thinner. A bit longer. Bloodless. Segmented. A hand with only thumb and two fingers. Talli stares, lone eye burning with dryness, as she will not blink. She watches the tiny hand as it grasps the sky-blue bedsheet, making a fist. Slowly, the sheet is reeled down past the far side of the bed.

She blinks. Tears come suddenly. Her gaze flicks to the tabletop. There sits a lump of iron pyrite, shining like purest gold. But she knows it will rust. She wanted to preserve it. Bring it south when she leaves. It was supposed to be a surprise for Meg. Now, Talli looks at it and thinks,

There's no gold in Avvajja. . . .

---

25 hours before lounge:

When her boots first touched the ground, she could only think,
There's gold in Avvajja!

She knew the countless lumps were iron pyrite, trash churned up by past mining. The stuff was everywhere, clots of sunny ore among Avvajja's oddly smooth rocks—sizes varying so greatly that stones like peas were cuddled up against those bigger than trucks.

On the twinkling gravel, Talli crunched along with Ambreen

striding at her left. Other than Talli, the dark-haired geologist was the only scientist in the group, making her an object of fascination for Drashtr. The latter watched Ambreen from where he rode on Talli's left shoulder, looking a bit like a pet Dungeness crab. Talli guessed that, later on, she would have to endure him laying out an entire personality profile based on Ambreen's body language. A few metres ahead of them, Troy and Ian walked side by side. It looked like Ian was doing most of the talking—no surprise—with Troy staring at the ground, hands in pockets. All around them was the former Avvajja mine, sixty kilometres west of Iglulik. Well, maybe. Talli was disastrous with geography. From the air, the mine had looked like a drained lake, three grey-edged, vaguely ovoid outlines, joined at a dark semi-circle that indicated the subsurface opening.

Once again, Talli coughed in the dry, Arctic air. Summer here, no snow, yet she could still see her breath. Unbelievable. This was where Ambreen should have reminded her that, as recently as the 30s, the Arctic was classified as a desert (or was that geography?). But the pale geologist marched like a machine, not bothering to ask Talli if she was well. Talli was not even sure what the girl's voice sounded like. Ambreen and Troy had kept to themselves from the time their airship had departed from a sea platform near Kimmirut. Ian certainly had "talked," but only to name-drop and propound about his Arctic experiences.

Long ride, Talli thought to herself, *but we're here: Charlie's Land.*

"We'll be in the mine, soon," said Drashtr. "Controlled humidity, there." His smooth voice spoke to Talli via her invisible earpiece. At once, his four crablike legs loosened against the styled layers of her dun jacket. With typical agility, he scuttled to a position where at least two of his four poppy seed eyes (arranged in a diamond) could catch her left eye. He shone in the sunlight, looking like a crab-legged mushroom cap of opal and pearl.

I'm a science pirate, she thought for the hundredth time, *complete with parrot. . . .*

Talli looked up to the edges of the mine. Beyond, she could see treeless hills in every shade of brown, purpled as though with titan brushstrokes. Flowers, probably. A big crow—no *raven,* she remembered from her research—coasted and tumbled in the chill wind. Here and there, the beauty of the place was compromised by some blue or orange polygon: garbage associated with the former mine. But it still seemed tragic that they were descending. She was seized by an urge to hike. To see what lay beyond the hills.

"You're thinking," said Drashtr, "so, this is where my ancestors lived."

"I'm thinking . . . Meg was wrong," Talli lied. Drashtr was synced to all her devices. Between the vibrations of her speech, combined with his talent for lip reading, she could speak to him in less than a whisper. "I should have done this by virtual."

"If you'd used vi," said Drashtr, "how would I arrive?"

"I'd have left you in a case," Talli smiled. "And had you pre-delivered, with the rest of the kit."

"Thoughtful," said Drashtr.

"I'm kidding."

"Me, too."

Drashtr was right, of course. She *had* been thinking of her ancestors. But, were they really hers? They had been the ancestors of Uncle Sarrli ("Charlie," as Aunt Abby had called him). Charlie had made the most of all the cultural stuff, with his survival-endurance-heritage-blah-blah talk. But even Charlie had lived most of his life in big cities. As a girl, Talli had been amused by his little camping tricks: always knowing north, building fires, customizing all his equipment. She'd loved the trips. And they'd caught a lot of fish together. But Talli was pretty sure that didn't count as "living off the Land."

As a whole, she tried to take in the sheer weight of the Arctic around her. The strange gravity that lent it a special life.

Charlie's Land, she thought again.

Talli shook her head, fighting a sudden funk. For a moment, it was as though wet clay had been packed around her heart. She had actually felt depressed.

Drashtr shifted on her shoulder.

Golden gravel crunched. Soon, the sun disappeared. They walked under the shadow of the massive "hood" arching over the mine entrance. As the road descended, structures appeared several metres to Talli's flanks—toothed edges, fluting, curves and planes of unknown materials. This had once been a colourful place, but scars from heavy machinery had turned it into something like an urban combat zone.

There was far more walking than she'd expected. Increasingly, they relied on anaemic lights, set without any obvious pattern or symmetry, in crannies beneath the hood. Ahead, the road ended in shadow. A wall? Some entrance had to be at left or right. There had to be an elevator. Like Troy and Ambreen, she stepped with confidence. But her eyes flicked to Ian, checking that he still seemed to know what he was doing.

Ian was a couple of decades older than the rest, maybe in his early fifties. He had supposedly spent some time in Avvajja after operations had shut down. When two robots, looking a bit like strawberry-layered, Millefoglie wedding cakes the size of dogs, popped up and flashed, Ian gave both a quick salute. He turned, grinning, amused at his own wit.

"Don't be alarmed, all," he said. "Levels and levels of security. Already looked us up and down from the time the airship arrived. If you weren't registered as visitors, they'd have mentioned so."

Talli hadn't been alarmed. According to international convention, it had been illegal to keep harmful bots inside of territorial waters since . . . the 50s?

Time of Mum and Dad's accident, she thought.

"Let's go, let's go," said Troy. "Fucking freezing, here. You could drink whiskey with my balls. . . ."

Talli frowned, not understanding.

Oh, she thought. *Ice cube equals testicle. Basal reality via genital comparison. Classy.*

Yet Troy did appear to be cold. His bared teeth looked like clashing rows of mints. A poof of sandy hair bobbed with the chattering. Ochre facial skin was contorted over the most symmetrical bone structure Talli had ever seen. While she and Ambreen wore modestly fashionable jackets (maybe Ian thought he was fashionable, too), Troy alone had opted to go coatless. His decaled trousers were Third World inspired and meant for southern autumns. His top was like the upper half of a skater's bodysuit. Talli could understand why he would want to parade that body. He—along with maybe parents, but more likely genetic engineers—had clearly worked hard for it. In the Arctic, however, vanity seemed to cost in a different way. She felt terrible for him.

Let him use my coat 'til we're in? she thought. They couldn't be far from an entrance.

Talli jumped, jostling poor Drashtr, so that he gripped tighter and pinched her. There had been a sudden noise: thunder, as the wall ahead slid downward.

A hatch.

Ian walked toward her. His mouth was working, but with the hatch still opening, she could hear only thunder. Talli ran a hand through her short, tangerine hair, grabbed her right earlobe and wriggled it back and forth.

Um, I can't hear?

Ian stopped in front of her, still talking, then looked startled, understanding. He adjusted his olive coat, tried and failed to smooth back grey werewolf hairs over his ears. The hatch fully opened and went silent as he pointed at Drashtr.

Talli looked back and forth between Drashtr and Ian.

"I'm not so sure about that," the man said. "Devices are fine, but if your bot could wait on the surface . . . ."

"He's no bot," Talli protested, trying not to sound snippy. "He's a *danseur* and I need him for my research."

That's what Meg and herself had agreed she should say.

"Danseur?" echoed Ian. He squinted, rotating an index fingertip in one ear. "Well . . . po-tay-to, po-tah-to."

"Sorry, no," Talli answered. "Bots are made of parts. They're machines. Danseurs are grown from little builders. He's whole orders above a robot, and I believe that Kralc U. already cleared him with your employers."

Bastard, she thought. *We messaged each other about this. For months!*

Features stony, she reached for the band on her wrist. "I can show you an attached permit from—"

"Goddamn, Ian!" yelled Troy. "Dad's gonna know you made me freeze!"

Ian's face turned ashen.

He smiled, returning to his usual mode of "nice old man." The same finger that had pointed accusingly at Drashtr (and gone wax mining) now curled at the danseur, as though air-tickling a baby.

"Well then, welcome to Avvajja, little guy," Ian told Drashtr. "This must be a grand adventure for you."

Out of the corner of her eye, Talli spotted rainbow hues shimmering over Drashtr's skin. Plain lines. That usually meant something like:

Asshole.

Ian grinned again, nodded to Talli, then turned back to the mine entrance. With Troy and Ambreen at his sides, he walked down to whatever lay beyond the hatch.

Talli watched them for a moment, eyes darting to a glint of gold at one side of the road. A particularly large chunk of pyrite. She jogged over, snatched it up: a gold cluster the size of her fist.

"It's just fool's gold," said Drashtr. "Rust if you bring it below."

"Pretty, though," muttered Talli. "And there's always a way to preserve things."

"But preservation implies change," said Drashtr. "More concepts. More conditioning."

Not this again, thought Talli. *The whole ride over. . . .*

Talli had travelled with Drashtr before, but on this long airship journey, he'd grown uncharacteristically anxious as they'd approached Avvajja. Could danseurs feel true anxiety? Or boredom? They had no central brains, Talli knew, but "thought" and "felt" through the synergy of their collective mechules. Maybe Drashtr had simply grown bored on the way here, developing an idiosyncratic, philosophical streak. One way or another, he'd been droning on about the dangers of "conditioning." Of "haecceity" and "interiority." Of "becoming." At one point, she'd thrown a pillow at him.

Though it was an affect, since he didn't have lungs, the danseur sighed. "You're thinking," he said, "here's Drashtr: droning on."

"No, no," argued Talli, hefting her pretend gold, "just appreciating what a ball of chuckles you are."

Drashtr shuffled on her shoulder. "Tal," he said, "please . . . be careful. You're at play. I'm already at work. I'm built to sense them, but not heed. To have neurons is to actually *hear* their song."

Talli frowned at these last few words. "Their what?" she asked. "Whose . . . did you say 'song?'"

First, Drashtr the philosopher. Now, poet?

"Others await," he said.

Talli wondered what he meant by "others," until she noticed that Ambreen, Ian, and Troy now stood in the open hatch, gesticulating for her to follow. Troy yelled a couple of indistinct words that did not feel like blessings. The young man seemed odious, constantly alluding to the notion that everyone wanted to sleep with him, yet Talli still felt a pang of guilt. He'd already stated that he was freezing. Yet here she was, making him endure further cold, while she'd wandered off like some small child at the sight of ice cream. Standing here with her lump of "gold," she suddenly felt exposed, unprofessional, ashamed at her own selfishness.

"Well," muttered Talli, trying to scavenge humour from the situation, "no one can resist free gold."

"And further conditioning," said Drashtr.

Danseurs weren't always cogent.

22 hours before lounge:

"Tal, just let them be," Meg told her.

"But you should see these people," answered Talli. She was hurt that Meg, who never seemed to care about the like or dislike of people, didn't get it. "Past teams, at least there's *somebody* I get along with. These people won't even talk. Not even to each other, most of the time. Un, un, unhealthy."

"Not everyone grew up like you, Tal," argued Meg. "That's Charlie's influence. You always want to bring everyone together. A lot of people enjoy keeping to themselves."

Meg spoke from Talli's "lampion," a sheet device thinner than paper. It was spread on the wrinkly bed, where Talli sat talking. Meg's image—the rich, dark skin of her Indian subcontinental heritage, with hair like black rivers of vinyl, and fashionably violet iris tint—smiled up at Talli in bas-relief. A partial hologram. Drashtr walked along the nearest wall of the tiny room, inspecting its vents.

"Not everybody," Talli answered.

"Well, why so fascinated with these three?"

Talli sat, unable to answer. It seemed like a fair question. Why had she felt so needy, grabby, *gooey*, since the airship landing? She nauseated herself.

"Talli," interjected Drashtr, "is a very empathetic person. Hence our love for her. Perhaps, in this place of her, shall we say, heritage, she's simply become more . . . herself."

Talli smiled at Drashtr's theory. It reminded her of something Charlie used to say of the Arctic:

People go there to become more of what they are.

Meg rolled her eyes.

"Besides," Talli said, "it's normal for teams to—"

"Drashtr," Meg interrupted, "can you explain to Tal she's not on a team?"

The danseur took a moment to join Talli on the bed, climbing the dangling sheets like a small action hero.

"Hm, technically," Drashtr told Meg, "Talli and I are a team. She knows the other guests have separate agendas."

"There's my bro's personality again," Meg said with a sigh. "You're going to position opposite to whatever I say, aren't you?"

"Natural, imitating my designer," said Drashtr.

"Let's not talk about that," Meg said.

And I've got issues? thought Talli.

"Have you found any listening tech?" asked Meg.

"Not so far," Drashtr answered. "Someone could monitor the ambient, I suppose, but the mine is old. The technology here is archaic. Not to mention cheap."

"Has to be a speaker nearby," said Talli. "That music's making me spun."

Silence.

"I don't hear anything," said Meg. "Drashtr?"

The danseur hesitated before answering. "There is," he said, "no music."

Talli's frustration shifted to anger. She found it hard to believe that Drashtr, at least, couldn't hear the sounds—faintly rhythmic with variances—that had been obvious in every quiet moment since riding the multiple elevators that had swallowed them down to the mine's former barracks. Talli couldn't make out any voices. But it was like hearing a group of people whispering the barest song.

Did Drashtr actually just lie?

"You cannot tell me," she told the danseur, "you don't hear that."

"Hear?" asked Drashtr.

"It's . . . I don't know, people chanting. Humming or something. Low voices."

Drashtr was silent.

"I don't like being dismissed," said Talli.

"Guys," said Meg, "stay on target, please?"

"By you, either," said Talli.

Meg made the face reserved for realizing she'd reached a limit with Talli, and said gently, "Tal, I love you. But the other guests don't—and that's okay. They have that right. Let them do their . . . whatever they're there for."

"Ambreen," Drashtr noted, "is here to study plate tectonics. Troy is the owner's youngest son. Probably wonders how he'll sell the mine."

"Like I said," Meg stated with a bored expression, "whatever they're there for. Look, Tal, Drashtr does all the work. You just babysit. Then you're back and we party. We look at the data. Party some more. 'Kay?"

"It's not healthy, nobody talking," Talli muttered. "I want to lounge with them."

"Leave them alone," sighed Meg.

"One lounge," Talli argued. "Maybe they won't even want to participate."

Anger flashed in Meg's violet eyes before she softened and shook her head. "Okay," she said, "one." Her eyes flicked to the side, where she fiddled with her own lampion. "But I get to pick the environment," she told Talli. "I just sent it. Your choices are always too spun, Tal. The one I sent is calm but aesthetic. Politically neutral."

"Whatever pleases Your Majesty," Talli said, noting the download.

"I'm anything but pleased," Meg answered. But her eyes were worried now, as though she were concerned that she'd pissed Talli off. It made Talli feel a bit better, but also a bit guilty.

As though she'd heard that her favourite cosmologist had passed away, Meg adopted a morose expression.

"What is it, she-creature?" asked Talli.

"I just broke the first rule of this venture, that's all," answered Meg. "No uploads or downloads."

Paranoia, again, thought Talli. *Afraid her research is going to get stolen.*

"We shouldn't even be talking," Meg went on. "Our contract demands University network use. Else we risk audit. Repeat: audit? What if some seventy-year-old IT creep, living in a closet on campus here, reports us?"

"We're pirates, I know," said Talli. But she was smiling.

"You and Drashtr," grinned Meg, "say, 'Ahrrr. . . .'"

"Ahrrr . . . ," said Talli and Drashtr together.

"Speaking of piracy," Meg said after a moment, face becoming hopeful, "Drashtr, anything so far?"

"Shit, Meg," said Talli, "we haven't even counted our bags yet."

"I did," corrected Drashtr. "While you were showering, Talli. All thirteen accounted for."

"How'd you do that?" demanded Talli, glancing at the heavy door. It wasn't that the bags were important. Most of their "kit" was crap, stuff to convince Kralc and Avvajja that they were doing what they'd stated in proposals. Drashtr was the active scientist, here. And the true equipment.

It was just that the door was locked. And Talli had no memory of leaving it open.

The danseur used a crab leg to gesture toward the vents along ceiling and floor. "Things open easily, here," he said.

"Seriously, Drashtr," pressed Meg. "Anything?"

"Much more than 'anything,' Meg," Drashtr answered. "The activity down here is rich. I can only imagine if we went lower."

"Really?" said Meg and Talli simultaneously.

"My mechules," he told them, "are responding to allons at a rate comparable to lab."

Allons were thought to be subatomic particles. A few advanced strains of mechule, even some comprising Drashtr, actually contained them. But unless so bound, they were fleeting things. Studying one was like trying to untangle a knot of unrivalled complexity by observing only its shadow. Upside down. In a mirror. Maybe while brushing one's teeth. Scientific dogma stated that such phantasms sparked into and out of reality, catchable only within the lab. Privately, however, Talli and Meg had begun to wonder about the large-scale influences of allons. This whole trip was about traceability in the patterns of nature—research for which, had they been honest, they'd never have received a grant.

What, Talli wondered, *would my ancestors have thought?*

Then, acidly, she wondered why she'd wondered it. *Which ancestors? The Irish? Or the bits of Cree or Scottish or whatever that sneaked into my genetic henhouse?* No, of course, she'd been thinking of Inuit. Because of Avvajja.

Of Charlie.

"As allons stimulate allons," Drashtr went on, "my mechules can sense a high—"

"Impossible," snapped Talli. "Natural activity would be subtle. You're contaminated."

"No," Drashtr insisted. "I think there's an exotic factor. A stimulant."

Meg ran a hand up her forehead, saying, "Please don't tell me we're going to have to junk this trip."

"Meg," groaned Talli, "come on. . . ." *Always the catastrophic view,* she thought.

"I'm not going to be able to sleep," said Meg, "till you isolate it."

"Like Talli pointed out," answered Drashtr, "we've just arrived. I still have operations pending."

Drashtr and Meg talked some more, skirting research particulars like a pair of spies. But Talli hardly heard. Her eyes lingered on the face (what Charlie would have termed "desktop") of her lampion. An icon. It had been there for some time. Untouched.

Delete? she wondered.

"Tal, you okay?" asked Meg. "Drashtr, she staring at the icon again?"

Neither Talli nor Drashtr replied.

"Tal, just delete it," Meg urged. Her violet eyes were suddenly filled with tragedy. "2077 minus 2064 years. There's a reason you haven't opened it."

And a reason I kept it, thought Talli.

"I hate him for this," muttered Talli.

She despised Charlie for blocking off her love of him. How could she love someone who had made cash from his own ruination? His own death? It had been trendy around the time her uncle had fallen ill. Untreatable pandemic of the time. Ulceration of the bowels. Virus that hid in neurons, defying vaccination. But don't worry—an experience like that has got to be worth something! Sign this contract and our production team can record your misery, your despair, your spicy, yummy corrosion, for billions of bored motherfuckers to enjoy via virtual. Stream it to the moon! Enshrine it as a download! You're not unwell—just commodified!

"He got you through school," Meg said. She went in that direction every time this came up.

A lot of school, thought Talli. *But without him.* She realized that she was pinching the edge of the lampion between thumb and forefinger, as though pinching Charlie.

She and Aunt Abby had hardly spoken since Charlie's death. His will had left money for Talli, though it had taken her some time to use it. He'd left the matches, too, one of the very boxes that used to come along on their fishing trips. Wherever she slept, the box was always by her bedside. She even knew why it contained two matches. Charlie-think.

Just the two of us, as he used to say while fishing.

And he'd left death. Like a dead bird at the base of a window. The log of his last days. That which had made the bucks and been available for the world to enjoy. Talli would have felt no less disgusted had he left her a favourite porn. But Abby had defended the decision, stressing that there were "things" Charlie had wanted Talli to know.

Things to know?

Like palsy? Fever? Hallucination?

The feeling of being pinned, as though by a predator, writhing as one's abdomen was pinched and torn?

Or reflections on foolishness, from a man's badly planned life?

Meg often said of Charlie's experience, "I don't want you

knowing that stuff." And she was right. If Talli opened that file, synced to the right device, her own neurons would virtually inculcate Charlie's final time. His deeds. Words. Even his feelings.

No.

But she didn't delete it.

---

12 hours before lounge:

Talli stood at one of three entrances to the dining area that had been reserved for guest use. Like her room, it was small: two tables with accompanying chairs, three abused loveseats and an attached kitchen.

Both other guests, plus Ian, were present, but all seemed glued to their own lampions. Based on plates, cutlery, and carrion, they'd eaten breakfast. Talli supposed that it was unreasonable to have expected them to wait for her.

At least, she thought, *no one joined me in the communal shower.*

Troy kept barking out laughter at his lampion, not bothering to look up as Talli entered. Ambreen stared sternly at her own, fingers flitting like moth wings over its face. Ian read with a blank expression.

"Better sound out," muttered Drashtr. Once again, he clung to Talli's shoulder. He looked a bit strange, today. Bumpy, like a few pimples had developed. Danseurs could will a slow change of shape, redistributing their mechules—the so-called "little builders"—over time. It made Drashtr useful in the lab. A living toolkit. But he didn't want to talk about this new bumpiness. When she'd asked, he had gone on about allons and operations. When she'd pressed, he had simply answered, "Hopefully, none of it will be necessary." She was hungry, so she'd decided to bug him later.

"Um, morning!" she called.

All looked up. Annoyed expressions.

This again, she thought.

"Ah, I thought it would be nice," she said with a strained smile, "if we get to know each other. I'm setting up lounge tonight?"

Troy: scornful.

Ambreen: insectile.

Ian: bemused.

"I . . . sent invitations to general Avvajja messaging," she told them. She had not yet received any responses.

And still did not.

Nobody checked messaging, she realized.

"My thesis advisor sent me a great environment," Talli lied, not having experienced it, "and I thought, oh, eight-ish? Tonight?"

"This is bad," said Drashtr, noting the lack of response. "Cancel the lounge. Before it's too late. Look at them, already on their way. One can't predict what these kind will become."

"You're just like Meg," Talli whispered, not entirely understanding his comments. "Go and think the worst."

"And you," said the danseur, "are conditioned. I am not. I see them as they are—not as reflections of my own conditioned mind."

The words stung. Sort of. Talli suspected that, somehow, for the first time ever, Drashtr had insulted her. Maybe. He could say awkward things. She'd unpack it later.

Talli broke eye contact and made her way to the fridge. Hopefully, no one had eaten the yogurt Meg had made for her. Though she had spoken to Meg only the night before, they'd agreed to a silent period, so their research could not be monitored. Talli's lampion was now reshaped, made into a band around her left wrist. She touched it as she walked, once again hating that she could never stand isolation. Meg never minded it. She could distract herself with work, always seemed to expect the same from Talli. And Charlie had always argued that independence equalled strength. But then, why had he always brought Talli fishing?

Drashtr was here, at least.

Talli froze as she reached for the fridge door. On top, there sat what had at first appeared to be a doll. It was pearly, like Drashtr, but had two arms, two legs, and an overlarge head. There were few other features, as it was like a figure shaped from wax or dough. Blank face. Eyeless. The vague points atop its head reminded Talli of a cat's ears.

While Talli watched, the "doll" flashed with colour, the entire visible spectrum storming across its surface. Then, doughy again.

Before Talli could speak, Drashtr flashed similarly.

"A danseur!" Talli breathed, trying to keep her voice low. "Isn't it?"

"Its name," said Drashtr, "is Aki. From the language of your people. In Inuktut, it can mean 'exchange price,' 'gift,' 'barb,' even—"

"I don't have a people," Talli hissed. "You and Meg are my—"

"That's been here for a while," Ian sounded from across the room. "Never talks."

"It talks a lot," muttered Drashtr. "But in circles."

"Appears here and there," Ian went on, "but no one ever sees it walk. First time I've known it to flash like that."

Talli looked over to Ian, who wore a bored expression on his face and had not bothered to rise from his reading. Troy and Ambreen had not even looked up from their lampions.

"How'd it get here?" she asked.

Ian shook his head, picking at an ear hair. "Lot of spec about that," he said. "No record of the company buying danseurs. And I'm glad. They're creepy. We think a research team left this one, maybe thought they'd come back for it."

"He's right," Drashtr muttered. "But they had no desire to reclaim it."

A team? wondered Talli. She restrained herself from interrogating Ian. Why would some other team bring a danseur down here? No one could have paralleled what she and Meg were doing, or Drashtr's role in it. Could they? Too bad no one was interested in lounge. It would have been the perfect venue for question and answer.

Yet she had to at least ask, "Did you, uh, host for that team?"

Ian gave a sudden yank, pulling a hair from the outside of his ear canal. He held it up between thumb and forefinger, squinted, smiled in triumph. He went back to his reading.

Talli got the message: *I don't answer to you, sweets.*

"Drashtr, could you ask, um, Aki . . . ?"

"Already did, Tal," said Drashtr. "It's acutely cryptic. But it has given me a lot to consider."

Talli sighed, turned from fridge and danseur, her mind suddenly on work. The first thing to do was cancel lounge, then . . .

She froze as a vivid display caught her eye. Aki's entire skin rippled with hues, patterns moving too fast for her to follow. At once, she was aware of a particularly strong scent, as of baby powder. Talli recognized it from working with Meg and her brother, who had been a genius in the area of danseurs. It was the smell of builders. Stray mechules being shed.

Within seconds, Drashtr seemed to imitate Aki, responding with his own rainbow spectacle. Talli stood confused as the two danseurs spangled at each other. But after several seconds, they simultaneously stopped.

Talli stood for a time, gaze flicking back and forth between danseurs. Both were silent. Still. And something was off about them. She eventually noticed that their textures had become matched. Both, instead of being smooth, now evidenced skins that reminded her of plucked birds. The sides of their bodies had grown tiny spines. It was like looking at a pair of pale lobsters covered in goosebumps.

Whispering, she asked, "What was all that?"

"A debate," said Drashtr.

Lounge:

To Talli's amazement, everyone showed up.

She had truly meant to cancel lounge, but developed an idea after watching the danseurs and their duelling hues (Drashtr was still evasive about it). She had simply left the dining area, saying nothing, leaving a mist of intrigue for all who had been watching. She'd guessed that, wanting an explanation, some would show up at lounge.

She'd been right.

After a long day of reviewing—sometimes correcting—particle animations on her lampion, Talli placed a slim collar (same tangerine as her hair) around her neck. It was synced to her lampion, a sheet again, which lay on her belly while she lay in bed.

"Later, Tal," she heard Drashtr say from next to her pillow. "Go put the fun . . ."

". . . in fungus," she finished with a giggly snort. It was an unfunny joke from a shared mycologist friend of hers and Meg's. Her neurons were getting spun from the initial touch of lounge.

Like anaesthetic, she always thought. *One, two, th. . . .*

(baby powder)

In lounge, Talli had taken some inspiration from Drashtr's opal, somewhat crustacean look. She wore a long dress made of interconnected, dreamily shifting arthropods: multitudes of tiny shrimp. Lobsters. Crayfish. Crabs. Too small and blended to individuate from farther than arm's length. Subtly coloured legs and antennae melded together into a soft spectrum, as when small rainbows appeared through mist on a sunny day. The neckline and sleeves of the dress were set to perfectly complement a purple obsidian necklace, with matching bracelets. She disliked heels, so her alabaster shoes were just high enough to make her feel dainty. Hair was often the most overdone thing in lounge, and Talli wanted this to be friendly, not competitive. So she opted for her normal hair colour, albeit extended into a long, somewhat Scandinavian braid trailing down her back.

Her fear had been that one or more of the other avatars would affect some silly, fantastic look (she felt bad for imagining Ambreen as a girl-sized mantis, Ian as a talking prostate, Troy as a turd). She couldn't stand it when people showed up as angels or monsters or celebrities, so she was relieved when all three guests appeared as themselves. Troy, who wore beautifully sculpted evening wear in glaucous greens and gold, had not changed a thing about his face or hair, except to wear pendulous earrings encrusted with emeralds. Ambreen came in a mulberry dress, red and ribbed like her shoes, hemmed to the knees. Its shape was wonderful, but Talli thought the ruby stars, winking from her outfit and high spirals of hair, looked a bit too matched. Ian wore a metallic, gunmetal suit over a silky magenta shirt. Talli was certain that, maybe two or three decades ago, it had looked dashing.

As her avatar walked into the heart of the lounge, she wished that Drashtr had participated. Danseurs could not actually lounge, but could experience it a bit by monitoring human neural activity. Drashtr, however, had "operations" to perform. It made sense, she supposed. He was the one doing the real work. While she lounged with the others by virtual, he lay beside her, combing through his own mechules, investigating the way in which their subatomic constituents were influenced by—or influencing—allons.

Meg's lounge environment was good. Titled *Flyting*, gold was the theme: a series of vaulting halls and chambers connected to a central hub, like a great, fat pillar, where Talli and the other avatars walked forward to greet each other. Everything here—ceiling, floor, every plane or curve of wall—was living, liquid gold, varying in shade or saturation as one stepped. It was as though they'd met in transparent vaults below a molten ocean, surrounded by metallic tides. There were no obvious lights, yet soft white fields floated randomly, so that shadows cast by exotic furnishings seemed to pirouette like idle children. It created zones, alternately afire or shadowed, like moving Rembrandt paintings.

Politically neutral, she thought, remembering Meg's description of the environment. *But* (as Charlie used to say) *like bannock without jam.* Maybe Meg was right, though. Talli's favourite environments, like, oh . . . riding cosmic dark matter webs or inside models of leptoquark loop materialization, might be a bit much for these folks.

Music! She could hardly believe it, but there was that whispered song again, like distant voices in a low, collective drone. She'd selected a watery, crystalline sound for lounge. It was present, but somehow combined with real world audio from the mine.

Should have Drashtr check my lampion, she thought.

Out of some peculiar sense of custom, a grinning Ian walked up with outstretched hand. Talli shook it, wondering why it was necessary, though she appreciated the courtesy. Ambreen gave a wave and simple, fleeting smile. Troy kept hands in pockets, staring at the floor to let everyone know that, by his standards, this was a "hillbilly" environment.

"Good evening, sweets," said Ian. He chuckled, then frowned a bit as she squeezed his hand quite hard. "I've only been to a few of these virtual things," he went on. "Mostly for work. But isn't this just fit for a little princess like . . . ?"

Ian trailed off, looking to his right, where the chamber was more open. Talli wondered if something was wrong.

Ambreen and Troy had already noticed that which had distracted Ian, and stood staring.

They were not alone in this environment.

Though Meg had promised an aesthetic environment, various singularities had appeared. Hideous ones. Ian had been startled by one of them floating into his peripheral vision. It seemed to be a creature about the size of a bulldog, but its form reminded Talli of things that dwelled in the deep sea (there'd been so many documentaries, watched with Charlie and Abby). Translucent. A gigantic, butterflied gummy worm, vaguely resembling female genitals. The thing flapped and floundered through the air, folds moving like skirt hems in unseen currents. Because of the creature's translucency, only its insides evidenced colour: snarls of intestines. Finger-thin. Blood red.

Spanish dancer, thought Talli.

That was it—the critter from Charlie and Abby's old documentaries. This creature looked much like a Spanish dancer: a kind of sea slug that convulsed its florid way through the oceans. Except that this thing was not colourful. And it was huge.

"Now isn't that something?" muttered Ian. He beamed at it.

Sure, if you like alien vaginas, thought Talli.

Like Ian, Troy and Ambreen seemed riveted to their own respective creatures. Ambreen would not take her eyes off another floater, like a huge pufferfish without head or tail. It was an ovoid ball of yellow spines, spotted with crimson blotches, fleshy ends resembling puckered lips. The thing drifted, a balloon on a windless day, so that the geologist smiled in childish wonder. Talli watched as, out of one end, the creature extended a long, languid tongue, yellowed with streaks of plaque. It stroked Ambreen's cheek, leaving some of its mustard on her. The geologist closed her eyes in apparent rapture, as though she'd been touched by a beloved hand.

Has everyone lost it? thought Talli. She found it impossible to believe that these vi-creatures seemed anything but loathsome.

Troy's smile was mischievous, dark, as he gazed at a hooded figure standing between table and loveseat. The figure was tall, obviously lean even beneath its trailing black robe. There was a terrible stillness about it. If the thing owned actual arms, they were folded. Talli could not see much of the creature's head beneath the hood, though it was massive, disproportionate to its stalk of a body. The open hood showed inhuman flesh. Black of rotten bananas. Green and red, as of a nose blow into tissue. The only feature was a mouth. A Venus flytrap. But vertical. The mouth ran from what should have been a forehead to what should have been a chin.

As Talli watched, the hooded figure raised itself, like a ballerina going up on toes. In one fluid movement, it glided around the furniture to settle a couple of metres closer to the guests. The move made Talli shudder and avert her eyes—it had seemed that, under the black folds, the thing had scuttled on many tiny feet.

Meg, how is this not spun?

Talli stepped back and stood for a time, unsure of what to say. She could sense the vi-environment using its equivalent of sedation. Tamping down negative emotions. Allowing her composure.

She had returned to being ignored. For a while, that was good. It gave her a chance to observe. Get her bearings. Eventually, she became aware that all three creatures had settled, like satellites, each to a given guest—or perhaps that the guests had moved over to their respective favourites.

She was baffled, not having seen such a feature in previous environments. Avatar . . . pets? Traditionally, a participant brought his or her own vi-pet to lounge. Had Talli been expected to select one for herself?

Her eyes ranged about the great chamber. So far, she could only spot these three creatures. Even if she'd been spun enough to like one of them, they were all paired up with the other guests.

I should have checked the settings better, she thought.

Talli tried clearing her throat but was still ignored. She could hear the guests speaking, yet soon understood that they were only addressing the creatures. No sounds came from the vi-beings. But each guest spoke to their favoured abomination as though chatting with a trusted acquaintance.

"Just so," muttered Ian at his gummy, vaginal thing. By now, it had extended a translucent tube, like an audio piece into which the man spoke. "No one respects experience anymore."

Ambreen was farther away, but Talli could hear her softly asking, "Is that how I would do it?" Her puffer thing kept licking her face, criss-crossing it with yellow.

Troy was too far away, but Talli could pick up barks of nasty laughter.

Talli grew furious. She had wanted a nice evening. Pleasant. Classy. Her guests were turning the whole thing into what Charlie would have called a "piss pond." On top of it all, she felt betrayed by Meg, who had provided the perverse environment.

"Hello?" she called. "Hello! Everybody! Look, I'm going to disengage. You seem to like this, so I'll send a copy to general Avvajja messaging, 'kay?"

At least she'd grabbed their attention. All three guests now stared in her direction. Disapproving looks. After a moment, they glanced at each other. Troy shook his head. Ambreen and Ian sighed aloud.

They tore themselves away from their creatures and walked toward Talli.

Like kids going to church, she thought. She suddenly hated them for making her feel guilty, like a diva, for threatening to exit.

Yet:

Starting with talky Ian, the guests seemed to recall the concept of basic politeness. The mustard streaks had faded from Ambreen's face. Troy had stuffed his hands back in his pockets, no longer laughing. Formal chit-chat trickled.

Did you enjoy the ride here?

Get all your bags and kit?

So where are you originally from?

What did you want to become as a child?

And, like spark to flame, there was actual conversation—however stiff. The guests never ceased to glance, from time to time, at the creatures (especially their given favourites). But they at least recognized Talli's living pulse. Only Troy was blatantly rude, sometimes turning his back while others spoke, so that he could admire his robed figure. Talli was grateful, at least, that he was containing his usual comments about everyone wanting to do him.

I'm ruder than he is, though, Talli thought to herself.

She had acted like an attention-seeking child, when the others had simply wanted to immerse themselves in the environment. Had she not invited them here? Had she not manipulated and twisted their arms to make this all be? Why couldn't she have simply left them alone? Here I am! Don't look over there! Look at me! Look how hard I've worked to be here!

Why did it have to be all about Talli?

No wonder, she thought, *people don't want to be around me.*

She did a lot of extra smiling, to let the guests know that she was contrite.

The chatting branched. Like whitecaps of vapidity, forgettable subjects arose and fell in the ether. Talli's mind drifted, until she was able to pretend at calm. Enjoyment.

At last, Ambreen said, "But that's what makes Avvajja special. The entire Canadian Shield, if you include Greenland, is reflexive to this point."

Talli's amber eyes widened.

"That's called *continental drift*," smiled Ian, looking back and forth between Talli and Ambreen.

Ambreen paused for a moment, as though listening for nuts rattling in Ian's skull, then said, "Continental drift is in the same landfill with flat Earth. Or antibiotics before the phage Renaissance. For decades now, we've had AIs model plate tectonics for us."

"Um, me and M—I mean—my thesis advisor and I, an AI brought our attention to a model like that," Talli told her, speaking with great care. "The whole continent kind of . . . has swung toward Avvajja since the Cenozoic. Hasn't it?"

"Well, sweets, we *are* near the pole," said Ian.

"More than the pole," muttered Talli, keeping her eyes locked on Ambreen and trying not to let irritation show.

While Ian stood with neck sunken like an angry seagull, Ambreen shook her head at Talli's original question.

"Nothing 'swings,'" the geologist replied. "Only shifts. But natural forces have to account. This shift has been . . . singular. Since the Paleozoic. At least."

Talli wracked her brain to recall what the Paleozoic was.

That's . . . half a billion years, she guessed. More than 400 million years longer than she and Meg had noted. She would have confirmed it with Ambreen, but she didn't want to interrupt while the dark-haired woman was on a roll. Inwardly, Talli felt stupid for glossing over the geology. Drashtr was thorough. Maybe he'd simply not spotted anything noteworthy.

Ambreen's eyes drifted along Talli's dress while she spoke, as though the geologist were really talking to herself.

"That's why I'm here," she droned. "At Nothsa Tech, we noted some . . . never mind, it's just shop. Did you mention a thesis advisor?"

"No, no, what were you going to say?" pressed Talli.

"Yes," said Ian, straightening with hands clasped behind him, "we can keep up."

"Well, it's dull," said Ambreen, "but we noted some chronostratigraphic anomalies in Archaean rocks from the surrounding Shield. So, there was an urge to rethink this point, which had been dismissed. I'm interested in the deep mines." She shrugged. "Just placing gravimeters."

Talli tried not to smile.

Gravimeters won't reveal it, she thought.

Ambreen smiled and shook her head, saying, "Don't know why I'm such a gab. I just . . . this environment makes me feel good. Isn't that dumb?"

Then the geologist did the oddest thing. For Talli, it was almost as eerie as the vi-creatures.

Ambreen laughed—more of neigh, really, reminding Talli of a horse.

Ian laughed, as well. "This *is* a nice place," he said. "And I adore the silly play-animals." He looked to his butterflied gum-thing, which waggled its tube near his ear. "Especially this one," he whispered.

"For me, it's this guy," called Troy. The robed figure stood like a black pillar on the open floor.

Ambreen directed a loving stare at her spiny floater. Again, it extended its tongue.

Gross.

"Our investigation's vaguely similar," blurted Talli. Not only did she want to keep up the back and forth, maintain the flow of info harvest, but she dreaded a return to the lurid communion between guests and vi-creatures.

Suddenly, Talli was the hub of all gazes. Again: unfriendly.

Did something shift? she wondered.

A subtle vibration seemed to run through the environment, raising goosebumps on her skin, though there was no reason for such a feature to arise in vi. The annoying drone of the music intensified. The effect on Talli was as if something tugged at her. Or perhaps pressed? She suddenly felt as if she were trying to concentrate on a conversation in a loud bar, while some drunken friend nagged for money to buy a beer.

"You're the physicist, yes?" asked Ian. "From Kralc?"

"Sort of," winced Talli. "I'm with a particle physics . . . team. We noticed the same thing as you, Ambreen."

By now, Ambreen had taken a couple of steps back from Talli, toward Troy. Smiling, the geologist whispered something in Troy's ear. He laughed, eyes ranging over Talli's figure.

"Particle physics," noted Ian. "Shouldn't you be off smashing atoms or something?"

"I'm a theorist," Talli answered. Since only Ian seemed to be listening, she spoke to him. "Ambreen's right. This place is, well, singular." She sighed. Might as well keep going. "There's evidence to suggest that, as with the movement of galaxies, traditional natural forces don't fully account for Shield positioning. In other words, the shape of the continent."

Ambreen was now directing a dark stare at Talli, as though suspicious that a "foreign" scientist had crept up on her research. It was what Talli had feared.

She has dibs.

Talli began to gush, hoping that more explanation would get Ambreen to retract her claws.

"But geology's just a clue for us," she said hurriedly. "Our focus is on subatomic and spatial—"

"What's that have to do with a mine?" asked Ian.

Again, all three stares.

Talli drew in a breath. "Well," she said, "when quarks—never mind, um, elementary particles making up composite particles in atoms—decay, they become . . . look, think of the dimensions you know, 'kay? Height. Width. Depth."

"And time," added Ian. "Think you'd remember that, as a physicist."

"She probably isn't," muttered Ambreen. "*Thesis* advisor. . . ."

Talli inwardly winced, pretending not to hear. "The dimensions are just imagery," she said.

I hate this.

This was exactly the social scenario physicists dreaded: normal woodchucks demanding comprehensible explanations without math.

"Look," she went on, "in the 2050s, AIs developed some new kinds of math. Phutharc, for example. They helped solve some problems with observations of how one quark seemed to decay into another. Now, rather than think of subatomic activity in terms of particles, we can think of them as 'bundled' packets of dimensions, jostling to assort themselves in space."

"Any dimensions," Troy snickered, "where lingerie models ride dinosaurs?"

Talli swallowed, stifling rage. She'd heard worse mockery. And at least they were listening.

Talli gave a strained smile. "More like," she said, "billions of abstract 'angles' trending into subatomic nodes. As one trend shifts into another, its corresponding planes resolve into our space. Temporarily." She struggled to find woodchuck imagery. "The angles are like . . . little, fleeting . . . spirits."

It was a word she'd borrowed from Charlie.

"You study angles?" asked Troy. "Seriously? Who cares?"

Just all of goddamn nature, she thought. Between them, she and Meg had clamped onto the notion that "universe" might simply describe a point into which countless other universes (also nodes in themselves) angled. In this model, reality was static: "movement" was really relative to dimensional assortment. But then, they'd been partying.

She tried to level her breath.

"They're not really angles," Talli explained. "Think of a honey-comb—"

"Dad was right!" howled Troy, though Talli wasn't sure how any of this could remind him of his father. He turned. Hopped. Pumped his fist. "Got to get the HON-ey, lil' BON-ny!"

"Okay, sure," said Talli. "You're right. Got it exactly."

At least he didn't compare it to his genitals, she thought.

"So, what's your *angle*?" smiled Ian, trying to contribute a pun. But as he spoke, his eyes seemed a bit glazed. They were not simu-lating drinking, here, so Talli wondered what was wrong with him. *What was going on, here?* The more time that went by, the more the others seemed to become . . . lost in themselves. They reminded Talli of a phenomenon called "parasomnia." It was a sleep disorder that Meg suffered from, occurring most often when she was under stress. Meg would rise from bed, even stand, albeit in a wobbly manner, but be unable to remember the names of those around her. Or where she was. Her brain was temporarily trapped in "confu-sional arousal"—a state literally between sleep and wakefulness. The first time Talli had seen it, the parasomnia had scared the shit out of her. She'd thought that Meg was having a stroke.

For a moment, Talli thought that Ian was rocking side to side. But then she realized that he was leaning toward the vaginal crea-ture, which flapped its folds near his right ear. It was as though the man were listening.

Like a dying spider, her patience shrivelled within her.

"I'm here for a force," Talli said suddenly. Defiantly. She was sick of being mocked. Dismissed. And to hell with Meg's secrecy. "Not gravity," she said, eyeing Ambreen. "A new force of nature. As expressed through a particle we've dubbed allon, meaning 'other' or 'alternate' one." She directed her eyes to the golden floor, thinking,

Shut up, Tal.

At least she'd restrained herself from saying the most important part: that Drashtr already had allons incorporated into his design. That he was here not only to find more, but to formulate theories around how they affected his little builders—the mechules that served like conscious cells in his body.

Talli and the twins—Meg and her brother—had endured years of mockery for their theories.

"We've only caught them in the lab," Talli finished. "But we're going to prove allons have always been a part of our environment. They hide. But they've moved nature all along. They hide but we'll find them."

Why am I even talking? she thought. *What the hell's wrong with me?*

Ian chuckled.

"So, they're like you, then?" he asked.

"Excuse me?" asked Talli.

Ian leaned closer.

"No, I don't think I will," he said. "You don't think I know anything, do you, sweets? Because I'm not a high horsy scientist? But I know more than you think. You hid. But you're found. Your name is Tallituq. 'It Hides Itself.' In the language of your people."

"My people?" asked Talli, taken aback. And how had he known her actual name? Or the meaning of it? Had he somehow researched her? Planned this? Was this all a grand prank?

"My creature told me some things, too," smiled Ambreen. "You're from here. Partly. The Inuit. Those are your ancestors. That's the real reason you came. You want to see if you can connect with this place."

Charlie's ancestors, Talli thought on reflex. *Charlie's Land. . . .*

She stepped back from the three grinning guests, their pet creatures hovering near. Troy began to dance in small circles, chanting, "Oonga-boonga, oonga-boonga, oonga-boonga, oonga-boonga . . ."

Fury rose white hot in Talli's throat.

Burst at Troy.

"Shut your gravy pipe you home-style slice of shit."

It was the voice she'd developed while growing up in southern schools. Since seven years of age. Since her parents—mother Italian, father Inuk—had betrayed her by dying in a plane that should never have been authorized to fly. Since she'd been raised by poor Charlie. And Abby. Since she'd been betrayed a second time, with Charlie's death, and what he'd done *with* that death. It was a voice reserved for all the kids who thought she wore feathers. Or needed "special" education. Or had cannibals for ancestors.

Stillness.

The three guests stood with eyes wide. Shocked. Troy had petrified in mid-step. Talli knew that look. It meant: We should call the police or security or something. Talli was no longer a scientist. She was a feral native. She was going to pick up a bow and put flaming arrows into their covered wagons. It wasn't that she was part-Italian. She was, in their eyes, mostly Inuk. She was some kind of cave creature, straight out of the Ice Age and ready to thump good, civilized folk over the head.

After a long moment, a smile stretched across Troy's perfect face. "Well," he said. At once, he cupped his hands around the sides of his crotch, and Talli realized that he was bulging. Hard. His eyes stayed locked on her own, as he thrust his pelvis toward her.

"No ice cream for her, now," said Troy.

The guests burst into laughter, rallying close to each other, their creatures hovering near. Talli had become a pillar of rage. Loathing. Somehow, even shame. Her fingers were curled like bird claws. It wasn't Troy's exact words or behaviour that upset her, but rather the way in which the others responded to it: huddling, cackling, as in a juvenile locker room. Somehow, there was an understanding between the three—no, the *six*. And, though it was a phenomenon she sensed rather than observed, the vi-creatures were part of this . . . display. She was now convinced of that.

She wheeled, seeking an exit alcove for her avatar, guest sounds trailing into giggles behind her. Why had she not listened to Drashtr? To Meg? These people were inhuman. Insane. She'd been out of her mind to think that she could find common ground with them.

"They brought a friend for you, too, Talli!" called Ambreen behind her.

What the fuck is she talking about?

Talli turned, ready to holler out her thoughts. But her view of the guests was blocked by a figure. It was a man in baggy, cornflower clothes. Short. Lean. About her height. Skin the colour of caramel. Pomade slicked down black hair streaked with grey. Lines fanned the sides of his cheeks, like micro-canals gouged by tears. Round nostrils flared on a high-set nose dotted with gaping pores, between higher cheekbones. Epicanthic folds, layered with wrinkles, lent his amber eyes a tragic, even despairing, look.

"Charlie?" whispered Talli.

Then Charlie smiled.

And kept smiling.

And smiling.

Talli could feel the clamp of her throat, as she watched Charlie's lower jaw sink. And sink. His mouth filled, dark lips peeling, with lengthening teeth. In the span of three heartbeats, his tobacco-stained teeth grew to the length of her fingers. And when his jaw could sink no further, the teeth began to push against each other, moving outward like those of a camel. They gleamed with saliva, which poured from gaps edged with purple gums, saturating the collar of that faded T-shirt she knew so well. The one that, between holes burned by campfire sparks, read:

FISHIN' FOR GOLD

Talli could now hear some of the still-growing teeth. Cracking. She grasped at her throat, as though she could physically seize her own scream. She was dimly aware of the obsidian necklace coming apart, pieces rattling to the floor.

She took command of her own vocal muscles. Forced the discipline that had brought her through school. That had kept her aloft through life. She readied to repeat his name. To demand of this image what it was doing here.

Goddamn you, Meg, she thought. *Did you place this—*

That's when Charlie bit.

Too fast for her to recoil, his mouth covered her face.

There was only blackness. Stink of coffee. Tobacco. Shock.

Teeth tearing skin.

Tongue seeking her screaming mouth. . . .

Minutes after lounge:

"Tal?"

She awoke to darkness. Pain. Terrible sinus headache.

Baby powder.

"Talli, you're okay. I'm here."

Drashtr.

The danseur must have been monitoring her neural activity while he worked. Sensed that she was experiencing trauma. But then, many people were like sleepwalkers while they lounged, Talli included. Drashtr had probably noticed her twitching like a hooked fish. Cracked her out.

Still in bed, she went up on one elbow.

"Move slow, Tal," said the danseur.

"Drashtr," she groaned, "that environment has, that is, it's— never mind the right terminology—it's fucked."

Rambling, she made a sloppy attempt to explain what she'd experienced in lounge. While she spoke, lucidity gradually returned. She realized that the lounge had had a mild hallucinogenic effect on her. Perhaps not as bad as on the others. But, toward the end there, she'd been convinced that Meg had planned it all—even the grue-some Charlie-demon—just to torment her. But she knew (at least now) that Meg could never be so perverse. So what had happened? The environment had seemed to hold the power of a dream, a night terror, puppeteering even her feelings to the point where every nerve in her had labelled it reality. She actually shook as she described it.

Drashtr made no sound until she was finished.

"It was not the environment," he said.

Talli gave a humourless laugh. "Well, it sure didn't happen in the dining area," she said.

"It did," Drashtr corrected. "Rather, it happened throughout Avvajja. I was right, Talli. It's the conditioning. They respond to it. Just as space responds to the angles. It's why you can become so much, Tal. Much more than me. I can sense them in my mechules. But I *only* sense. You experience."

"You don't want this experience, Drashtr," she moaned, sitting up.

So sick.

"You can't stand yet," said Drashtr.

"Humans need to pee," she told him. "And maybe puke," she added after a moment. "Grab my lampion. Get it to shed some light in here."

"Already doing so," said the danseur. "It's right here, with me. You'll need it for—"

"What? Bullshit. I can't—"

"Your eyesight should return shortly," Drashtr explained. "Your left, first. I had to go in through the right."

"What are you . . . ?"

Panic. Her headache was on the right.

Talli's hand shot up to her right eye. A bit swollen. Rimmed with stickiness. No pain until . . .

Ah!

Tear duct near her nose. She pulled away something like wet fudge. A paste she could almost roll between thumb and forefinger.

Aging blood.

She could smell it now, copper barely covered by the baby powder scent.

My blood. . . .

Wondering if she were still in lounge, she twisted about at the edge of the bed. Scanning the room. Hoping to see something. Even a vague outline.

Blackness.

"Tal, just be patient. The only mechules I implanted are near your anterior insular cortex. Brain's empathic centre. Very safe."

Hearing Drashtr's voice, so near, on the bed, caused her to shoot out an arm toward him. She wanted to squeeze him. Demand an explanation.

Instead of Drashtr, her fingers plunged into a field of filaments. Wiry. Tickling. Kicking between her fingers.

That's not Drashtr!

A snarl of reflex brought her arm away from . . . whatever she'd felt, then caused it to scythe outward again.

The back of her hand hit something—the thing that had spoken as Drashtr—knocking it away. Within the same heartbeat, there was a thump. Wall by the bed. She'd sent the thing flying against the wall. The sound was followed by another thump, the same entity falling to the floor between bed and wall. And there was another sound. Scratchy. Parchment-like.

Her lampion? Had she knocked it away as well?

She groped at the surface of the bed. Felt only bedsheet. Talli could not bring herself to reach between bed and wall. She thought only to grope at the night table, where she always put her uncle's matches. Upon touching them, she finally vomited: a snappy, almost elegant puke, since she'd eaten little before lounge. It was accompanied by an absurd thought about the floor:

Not so green now, are you?

She got the matches, at least.

Passed out.

One hour after lounge:

Sound of distant music. She opens an eye.

Talli lies on the edge of the bed, where she collapsed. She knows this because she can see the outline of the door, finely limned with light from the hall.

Not blind? she wonders.

Talli realizes that the lights are off. In the room, anyway. Remembers.

Shut them off for lounge.

Her fingers are curled around a matchbox.

Charlie.

Her mind wakes.

Drashtr.

Stifling groans from lying in a twisted position (how long?), she rises quickly. Steps toward the door.

Talli puts her ear to the door. Like falling dust, her fingernails brush the handle.

There are sounds from the hall. Shuffling? Are the others somehow waiting for her out there? Stalking? She remembers them from lounge. Demon folk. She'll never trust them again.

Her lampion. She needs it. Probably on the other side of the bed. But Drashtr is there. She can smell the baby powder of his mechules. Or does she smell the other danseur? That Aki thing? Was it imitating Drashtr?

In the dark, her good eye unconsciously flicks up, down, toward where the vents would be. She can't see them. But she remembers Drashtr's words upon inspection:

"Things open easily, here."

Talli recalls what Charlie used to claim when camping: night vision comes faster after the eyes have been closed for a bit. Talli shuts her functioning eye.

Lighting a match. How does one do it?

She fumbles about, dropping the matches while Ian, Ambreen, and Troy call to her from the hall.

Charlie's trick is of little use in reclaiming the matches. But at last, she gets one lit. Enough light to spot the fool's gold lying on the table. She meant to preserve it. Give it to Meg. Now, she realizes that Drashtr is right. Just garbage.

She sees a danseur arm reach up from between bed and wall, grasping at the sheets.

"Talli . . . are you there?"

Drashtr's voice.

She doesn't answer at first, then asks,

"Are you Drashtr? Or Aki?"

She finds the iron in her soul. Whatever this little bastard is, she isn't afraid of it. She glares, one-eyed, at the bed, as the match lightly sears her thumb and forefinger. She drops it.

Yet she's still not in perfect darkness. She can now see weak, saffron light, shifting behind the bed.

Her lampion. Drashtr has it.

"Aki's dead," Drashtr answers. "It donated its mass to me. Such was the nature of our debate. We agreed that one of us had to modify ourselves. In order to best serve you. You still look good, Tal, if that's your worry. We only freed you on the inside. But you'll not recognize my new body."

Talli marches over to the table, seizes the golden lump. She wheels back to the bed, cocks her arm back into a throwing position. The lump is about as big as her fist. At age eleven, with Charlie at her side, her stone throws could shatter shale.

"Come out," she demands.

She winces. The mine's music grows louder. But she still can't make out any words.

"I'm already out, Tal," Drashtr answers. "And in. Please don't harm me. You'll need me. To go deeper. We're always a team."

Talli crosses the room and slams on a light. She realizes, as the white glare comes on, that vision is returning to her right eye. A bit blurry. Dizziness, nausea, also gone. There's a small mirror on the wall by the toilet. Criss-crossed with enough cracks to make it resemble sloppy tile work. Good enough. Moving in a fast burst, she steps toward the mirror. Her lungs work the air, readying to look at herself, then. . . .

Not bad.

Her right eye is fine. Near the nose, it's a bit red. But she's had worse from pollen allergies. Her eyelashes still bear some dark flakes. Dried blood. But she's not swollen. Or in pain.

She smooths down her bedhead.

Talli wheels back to the bed, ready to renew her insistence that Drashtr come out. She's decided not to kill him. Yet. Questions to ask.

The danseur has already emerged.

Talli stands breathless, taking in the beauty of him.

Like a little . . . god, she thinks.

Incorporating Aki's "donated" mechules, Drashtr's new body is larger. Size of a big cat. Still, he stands on four crablike legs. But the mushroom cap, once his whole body, is now something more akin to hips. Centaur-like, a humanoid torso springs from these hips, though it bears four segmented arms and no distinguishable head. Hundreds of tiny limbs project from "chest" and "abdomen." Like the limbs or antennae of shrimp. Talli realizes that they are what she touched in the dark. A few limbs are as thick around as a wedding band. Others seem thinner than hair. Most, she notes, display exotic protrusions, like toy surgical tools. A few are tipped with familiar, poppy seed eyes. Those of the old Drashtr.

Yet it is Drashtr's new colours that widen Talli's eyes. Hundred-fold hues drift across skin and chitin, across every millimeter of his form. They're like fast clouds. Flocks of parrots. Vivid as blood. Sun. He is alternately awash and feathered in constant colour.

And quite lovely.

And bowing.

To me?

At the danseur's feet, where he stands on the bed, Talli spots her lampion.

"Please," mutters Drashtr.

Talli knows what's on the lampion. She can see from across the tiny room.

She puts down the fool's gold.

Picks up the lampion.

Charlie's image is there. But not the demon Charlie. Not the vigargoyle. Not the tobacco-stained biter.

Just Uncle Sarrli. His simple smile. The child-brat-dreamer-seer in his amber eyes.

She sighs. She knows what Drashtr opened.

She can close it.

Delete?

"You are no longer conditioned," says the centaur-Drashtr. Easy as a cat, he leaps from the bed. His colours immediately imitate the green floor.

"I will contain your empathy," adds Drashtr, "until you need it again. It'll not serve you here. But I always will."

For a moment, Talli basks in his words. Not their exactitude, but the feel of them. Perhaps because of the alterations he has made to her brain, perhaps because his words seem to merge with the music of the mines, she can actually soak in his intent. She does not hear him, so much as sense in the way of breathing in a scent. Or visualize a texture by working it between fingers. And with this comes gnosis, flashing like distant lightning, but leaving her unable to fully articulate its veins and arterioles of meaning.

"My empathy," she mutters, almost to herself, "was what the allons bonded to. My conditioning. They found Charlie in me. . . ."

"Just as they plumbed the interiorities of the other guests," said Drashtr. "Your ancestors knew about this. And they singled out special people. Adapted individuals. Ones who could ride the allon surge. Use it. Understand what it does to less adapted minds. Though allons don't truly think, as such, they 'knew' you owned this potential, Tallituq. You might say they recognized you from the time you stepped off the airship. But you didn't have the training Charlie hoped you might have by this point in your life. So I've assisted. Neurologically. The allons should no longer seize randomly upon your empathetic qualities. It was . . . the best I could do. The best *we* could do. Aki and I."

Freeing me, thinks Talli, *to hear Charlie's message.*
About Avvajja?

"They're here for you, Tal," says Drashtr. "And you for them. You are the exotic factor. The stimulant. We all abide by what you decide."

The music, ever wordless, swells and subsides in her ears. She realizes, now, that it's accompanied by the sound of surf. She looks at Drashtr, then at the lampion.

She searches the room. Finds the devices she needs.

Seven hours after lounge:

Stomach growling, she leaves the room. The hall is now dark. She hears Drashtr's footfalls, pebble-like, beside her as she walks. To left and right, archways to the showers—gendered, non-gendered—loom like mouths of night.

Turning. More dark halls. Empty. All the doors are open.

She finds the three of them in the dining area. As before, they don't look up at her approach. Each one reclines on his or her favourite shabby couch, trying to stay as far away from the others as possible.

Talli walks along the wall, winding around chairs, until she reaches Ian.

Ian lies back, eyes closed, smiling, as though soaking in the sun. The lower part of his shirt is unbuttoned, so that his middle-aged abdomen protrudes without shame. The song of the allons is now like a translucency, a veil affecting all of her senses. Through this filter, she Sees what the allons have exteriorized of Ian's interiority. She sees the vaginal creature as it floats over him, its clear tube extended into the man's navel. The organ has stretched his navel wide. She watches, at last understanding what she sees, as the creature pulls Ian's intestines out through the tube. The movement is gentle, idle, like a child playing with milkshake and straw. She watches the intestines mingle with the creature's own, floating like dreams in its inner soup. Gently, they are pushed back into Ian's body cavity.

Talli feels a sudden urge: the desire to test Charlie's latest lessons.

"Ian," whispers Talli. "Where are you now?"

He answers like a sleepwalker.

"So sweet," mutters Ian, eyes still shut. "Too, too sweet. Did you know I've been recognized? They made me head of their most important Arctic council. Finally. They recognize gold when they see it! Can't keep up with the demand for my lectures. Someone still respects experience! So sweet, too sweet. . . ."

Talli winds around the room until she comes to Ambreen.

The geologist's spiky puffer creature still has its tongue extended. It never stopped licking. Ambreen sits upright, like an ancient statue, barely recognizable under coatings of mustard. Talli now notes that the mustard is made of many yellow eggs—almost too small to individuate. Handfuls of them are layered over Ambreen's upper body and head, concealing the geologist's face. They are thickest around the nose, over eyes, ears, and chin. What seems like a hump is actually Ambreen's hair. Talli notices, after a moment, that she is mostly looking at the shells of tiny eggs. Many are hollowed, having hatched. She has no idea where the former occupants have gone.

"Hi, Ambreen," Talli whispers. "Where are you?"

"Secure, thank you," snaps Ambreen. Clumps of egg-mustard fall away from her moving lips. "I have been taught stability. Symmetry. Perfect planning, execution, life. Compromise me? Destabilize me? What do you know about symmetry? *You're* still on your thesis. . . ."

Talli moves on as the puffer drifts closer, licking fast to replace the eggs that fell away.

Troy is in a shadowed corner. Only about half of his body mass remains. The hood has fallen away from his creature. It waltzes in half-circles around him, moving with great elegance. Like a gardener, it pauses from time to time, stoops, gauges what needs to be trimmed. The fungal head shoots out from its rubber neck, faster than the eye can follow. The vertical mouth trims another piece of Troy. There's little blood when it takes a mouthful, cloth and all. Each trim leaves tarry saliva. The stuff spatters Troy, sizzling on his wounds. He is already eaten to the pelvis. To the shoulders. The upper, forward quarter of his head is gone, leaving a tarry bowl of open sinus cavity. The ear lobes are there, though. Talli remembers them from lounge, when they sported dangling, emerald-encrusted earrings.

"Troy," Talli whispers.

"Here for ice cream?" calls Troy. His voice booms. "Never fooled me, baby-girl! Everyone wants a piece of this! Too late! I'm a fucking pyramid! Solid gold! Eye in the middle! Dad knows it now! Suck on my god parts! Ch-CHAK! Nobody ignores me. . . ."

Talli walks away as he raves.

She's just here for the last of Meg's yogurt. After a few hours in vi, with Charlie, *being* Charlie, she's starved.

When she's done, Talli drops the yogurt container and leaves. No backward glance. She now understands, appreciates, what Aki and Drashtr did for her. She recalls the contents of Charlie's life, a vivid vi experience enhanced by allons. It could have driven her mad, if Drashtr had not suppressed her empathy.

Talli doesn't feel the mechules he implanted in her brain. She only appreciates their effects. Emotional control. A lack of mental conditioning (the reason why she isn't bound to mental golems, like the others). Someday, she'll ask for her empathy back. But not in this place. Not until she uses Charlie's lessons.

As it turns out, Charlie taught very little on camping trips. Everything was preparation for what he wanted her to know. Heritage. Secrets, hidden by family over generations. Hidden by her people. Over aeons. He died before she was of an age to consciously know such things. But he did plan. Charlie was better at the long game than she ever suspected.

She needs to be here.

In this Land of secrets.

Amid riddles that even mining cannot unearth.

Talli's Land.

For the Arctic, she sees, is a place where people go to *become*.

More.

Of what they are.

Forever after lounge:

Drashtr as guide, Tallituq enters the deep mine. Like all life, her lineage is shaped by evolutionary forces. Including the one that coils below. She now knows the secret tongue of her ancestors. Singing, the allons rise to greet her.

Utiqtuq

Gayle Kabloona

ON THE SHORE OF A LITTLE LAKE ON THE WESTERN COAST OF Baffin Island, Aliisa stood with a handful of rocks. She dropped them one at a time through the thin ice forming along the edges of the lake. *Crunch-plop, crunch-plop*. She liked that sound, and besides, there was nothing else to do. Tonight was wet and kind of foggy. Aliisa looked west, over the lake, toward the sea on the horizon; it would freeze soon, too.

"Come on, sun, you can come out any time now." She shivered. This night shift felt long. The nights had been getting darker recently. The days of twenty-four-hour sunlight were ending, and as summer waned, the air became crisper.

She couldn't tell how long exactly she had been up. They had stopped telling time with hours a long time ago.

It's actually been years, I guess, she thought to herself. It didn't really matter, though; they didn't need to be anywhere at any particular time. No school nights, no alarm clocks, no mealtimes; they ate when they were hungry, went to bed when they were tired, moved camp with the seasons (or, more accurately, when Ittuq told them to pack up). Now that it was getting dark again at night, Aliisa took the overnight shift because her eyes were sharper in the dusky near-darkness.

Their year was defined by the seasons: times when they caught Arctic char in the rivers or lakes, times when berries covered the tundra, times when the sea ice froze and they could catch sunning seals. The dark, cold part of mid-winter and the glorious spring when the world seemed to open up. It had been three long, dark winters since they left town, left everyone behind. She'd be thirteen soon, her birthday coinciding with the horror that spurred their escape to the land.

They had camped near this lake by the coast for the summer, catching char with a boat Ittuq had fashioned out of some old, abandoned fuel drums. They caught fish, dried fish, and ate fish. All day, every day. Aliisa hadn't let on that she was pretty sick of eating fish. At least when she was on watch she could supplement her diet by stooping to pick berries or *qunguliit*, the tart little plant with a red tower of seeds they used to call "Inuk candy."

Aliisa adjusted the rifle on her back and started toward the little hill behind the tent where Ittuq and Anirniq were sleeping. If she didn't move around a little, she would definitely fall asleep, even if she was cold, and she didn't want to put them in danger like that.

There was a rock at the top of the hill the perfect height for resting on. She called it her leanin' rock. She had a pretty good vantage point from there. She scanned the area for anything moving, anything that could be eaten or that wanted to eat her or her little adoptive family. Nothing so far; only rocks, tufts of tussock grass, and little rivulets of water running toward the lake under a thin layer of ice. She listened to the water still gurgling under the ice over hidden stones. She could hear nothing else, not even a bird chirp or a bug buzz. The gloom cut into her field of vision, but there was still enough visibility for her to feel secure. Secure that if anything came out of the mist, she'd be ready for it.

Aliisa shuffled her rubber-booted feet and scooched against her leanin' rock. She found a comfortable place to rest and ran the fingertips of one hand against the rough lichen growing on the rock. She slipped into one of her many pastimes, absent-mindedly counting the rocks in front of her.

"*Atausiq, marruuk, pingasuuuut*"—yawn—"*sitamat . . . talli . . . mat . . .*" She began counting at one, but her mind drifted away as the numbers grew higher. Her eyes drooped closed. Her head fell forward.

She instinctively inhaled sharply as she started awake. *Ajai, whoa, Aliisa! Stay awake!!* She was blinking rapidly, wondering if she had nodded off for long, when she heard a distinct sound. Her breathing stopped as she listened, and she was suddenly alert. Footsteps. The rifle came off her back in one swift movement. Her ears trained on where the sound was coming from as it became more pronounced. Her suspicions confirmed, she hugged the rifle butt into the soft spot between her shoulder and chest. She moved the bolt up and back, bullet into the chamber, bolt forward and down.

She still couldn't see anything through the fog, but she was pointing her body in the direction of the sound. Her left leg was perched up on her leanin' rock to steady her left arm that supported the rifle barrel. The crunching on stones grew louder, closer. Now she could see the outline of a dark shape lurching grotesquely toward her. It was coming fast, but she didn't fire yet. She slowed her breathing, calming herself, willing her body to become still. Her forefinger depressed the trigger gently, but not enough to fire. Finally, she could make out the figure's outline—it was coming straight at her, fast. Her right eye placed the rifle sights on the silhouette's head and her aim swayed with its rapid movements, waiting for the perfect moment to fire. She waited until it was about thirty metres from her. She took a slow breath in and a slow breath ou—*CRACK—fwiiiip—thunk!*

The *ijiraujaq* flew backwards headfirst. Aliisa already had another bullet in the chamber but waited. The zombie lay on the ground convulsing, limbs flailing. But Aliisa knew it was a good shot. In a few more moments it would stop, its body convinced that the head was indeed dead. The last of the jerking slowed and stopped. She approached cautiously. She listened intently for more sounds and kept her finger on the trigger, just in case. She got closer, rifle ready, and kicked at the ijiraujaq's feet. No movement. It was, in fact, dead . . . or deader . . . whatever you wanted to call it. She drew back the bolt of her rifle and carefully pushed the spare bullet back into the clip. *One bullet, one body.*

She walked up the ijiraujaq's body to inspect the head. Her bullet had hit exactly where she'd wanted it to. There was an oozing cavern where its face used to be. Little bits of bone and black sludge were sprayed across the rocks behind the body. It wasn't like killing a game animal; this thing's blood wasn't blood anymore.

"Stupid dead bodies getting deader and deader." She glared down at it accusingly. "Quit running around trying to eat people, ugh." It looked like this one had gnawed off its own forearm and hadn't been picky about the jacket covering it. Aliisa was careful not to touch or step in any of the gunk strewn behind the body.

I guess we'll have to move camp now. Don't want to track this heap of contagious death all over the fishing grounds.

She pulled her jacket sleeve over her hand, carefully grabbed the ijiraujaq's foot, and dragged its lower body so the head was facing away from their camp. It was a hunting tradition. If you pointed the carcass of an animal toward camp it would bring you better luck; more animals would come to you. Except with *ijiraujat*, with zombies, they pointed the bodies away from where they lived. Might as well try, right?

Ittuq, meanwhile, had been jolted out of his sleep by the gunshot and had emerged through the tent's flap.

"Aliisa, *qanuinngilatit?*" he called. "You good?"

"*Ii, ijiraujaq qukiqtara.* Yeah, I shot an ijiraujaq. It got way out here. . . ." Aliisa started to reply.

Ittuq approached Aliisa and the mess on the ground. "This one must have been tracking us for a while," he explained, looking over the carcass. "We just need to clean up these stragglers and we should be okay," he went on. "The further north we go, the less we'll see. I know it doesn't seem like it now, but we will get somewhere safe eventually."

Ittuq saw the pained look on Aliisa's face. "Aliisa, you're doing great," he reminded her. "You're surviving. It's not your fault. You know you need to protect yourself."

Aliisa sighed. Ittuq was right, of course; it *had* gotten easier since the beginning. Although she still felt odd about ijiraujat. When she was holding her rifle, she knew it was her or them. But afterwards, well . . . looking down on them, she would start thinking of all the people she used to know. When the things were running and slobbering and scary her instincts kicked in, but she was still human after all. She missed her old life, and these things reminded her of where she'd come from. Since narrowly escaping Iqaluit during the pandemic, she had slowly come to terms with this new life. She had quietly slipped away one night after helplessly watching her family turn into ijiraujat. She'd had nothing with her and wasn't going to make it far when Ittuq found her, cold and distraught, far up along *Niaqunnguup Kuunga*, Apex River.

Ittuq had also rescued Anirniq, a toddler at the time. Who knows where the little guy came from; he hadn't said a word to either of them, ever. Ittuq had taught Aliisa how to shoot and survive, but even if they were already dead, every ijiraujaq reminded her of her loved ones after they'd turned—with crazed eyes, clawing hands, and biting at each other—but also before, when they were alive and loving. Her mind sometimes got stuck in a feedback loop. It was hard not to feel bad for these people and what they once were, in theory. But when confronted with a terrifying, decomposing, sprinting monster, those feelings didn't matter anymore.

"Don't go back into that place, Aliisa," Ittuq said, accurately assuming her train of thought as always. "How many times have I told you? You can't help them. You have Anirniq and me; now, don't we count for anything?"

Aliisa absent-mindedly rubbed her shoulder, a bit sore from the rifle recoil. "Yeah, of course," she mumbled.

Their conversation was cut short by a strange sound, one they hadn't heard in years. This was a big sound, a deep sound reverberating across the land. Their faces turned up to the sky, the sound growing louder as it neared. A chopper appeared in the sky through the faint dusk and grew more distinct as it flew toward them. They both stared in awe. *What the! Who was flying it?? Where did they find the fuel? Why were they here?* This was huge. Aliisa felt like planes and helicopters were from a different life. Even timid Anirniq, who usually cowered at the slightest hint of danger, poked his little head out of the tent to look.

The helicopter, a red one, quickly grew closer. They saw two helmeted heads looking back at them from the cockpit. Having circled around them once, the chopper set down on a flat patch between the tent and where Aliisa and Ittuq were standing. Aliisa squinted and plugged her ears at the noise, and Ittuq watched distrustfully. The two heads inside were busily doing whatever tasks a helicopter required after landing. When the rotor blades stopped moving, one of the heads exited. He came over toward the two Inuit, hand outstretched in Ittuq's direction.

"Doctor Robert English, medical doctor at the Coleman Research Centre for Communicable Diseases at the University of Toronto!" he called.

Ittuq stood stock still, looked at the tall man, and didn't offer his hand in return. The doctor put his down awkwardly. Aliisa stared open-mouthed at this tall man. It had been years since she had seen a *qallunaaq,* a white person. Even before they had gone to the land, as the pandemic became serious, most of the *qallunaat,* the white people, had left the North to be with their families in the south. This man's red survival suit was so bright and new it almost hurt Aliisa's eyes. Not a stain on it. Brand new boots, unscratched glasses, and so many gadgets hanging off him. She suddenly felt incredibly grimy. Everything she had on was the same colour by now, covered in dirt and old bloodstains.

"Do you two speak English?" the red-suited doctor asked tentatively. He looked strange and slightly uncomfortable. His immaculate little glasses perched on a huge, pointy nose. He had looked them both up and down and taken in the dead ijiraujaq to their left.

Ittuq nodded his head once. "Yeah," said Aliisa, meanwhile burning with a thousand questions she wanted to ask all at once. *I thought you were all dead.*

"Great!" the qallunaaq exclaimed. He looked relieved. "Well, I suppose I should explain what we are doing here. I'm with the ReNew Canada project distributing vaccines and treatment to survivors in the Canadian hinterland. A year ago, the CRCCD developed a vaccine for the virus that decimated 86% of the population. We began treating the infected, and the vaccine has been quite effective in preventing infection in healthy individuals. All survivors of the pandemic must be relocated to regional treatment centres set up around the country. It was communicated that some Inuit went back to the land to escape the infection. I, along with Greg here,"—he motioned toward the pilot approaching—"have been tasked with rounding up the remainder of you and bringing you to Igloolik, where triage will assess you. You'll then be transferred to Hamilton, Ontario, for quarantine or placement in the required remediation group. Now, can I get your names please?" A notepad had appeared out of one of his suit pockets, pen poised to officially record their existence.

Aliisa stared agape at this man and his pilot. Everything was okay now? They could go back to living in a house again? With TV? And a PHONE? Her mind started racing: couches, snacks, food other than seal and fish, showers! School! *Wait. Ew, school. . . .*

I wonder who else is in Igloolik and Hamilton. Had anyone she knew escaped?

"No," Ittuq said, startling Aliisa out of her daydream.

The doctor raised his eyebrows. "Excuse me?"

"I said 'no.' We are not going with you," Ittuq said, this time louder. He had adopted a stony-faced look, one Aliisa had never seen before.

"I . . . uh . . . I'm afraid you are required to," the doctor replied. "The entire Canadian population must be treated and vaccinated to prevent another outbreak."

"I'm not leaving this land!" Ittuq almost yelled, pointing to the ground at his feet. "We barely escaped town with our lives and now you want us—no, you ORDER us to go with you?! Every time the government has interjected into our lives, it gets worse! Just let us be! It's too dangerous to go back, and I won't!"

At this outburst, it was the qallunaaq's turn to stare wordlessly. Aliisa looked back and forth between Ittuq and the doctor's shocked face.

The doctor quickly pulled himself together and looked to Aliisa, deciding Ittuq was the definition of crazy and that she was in charge now. He was all business again, ignoring Ittuq completely.

"Um . . . maybe I should explain a little more. Let me get my equipment." He forged ahead with his captive audience, Aliisa, while Ittuq stood in the background, scowling. The doctor went back to the helicopter and retrieved a laptop bag and a small cooler. He set them down by the tent.

The doctor was trying to set up his laptop on a rock, but it wasn't working so well. He was trying to even out the surface to keep the laptop's screen level. First, he put his notebook under one side, a few Kleenexes, then a flashlight . . . which rolled out from under it, and the laptop almost fell off the rock. "Oh, for God's sake," she heard him mutter. He didn't look like he was used to being outside in the wilderness.

Aliisa suggested he put it on the cooler, but that made the doctor more frazzled.

"No, no, no, I'm going to need that. This is fine, it's fine." In the end, he settled on perching the laptop on the rock, slightly askew. He clicked around a bit on the trackpad and brought up a PowerPoint presentation. Greg had joined, standing silently behind him. The doctor launched into listing a litany of medical facts, percentages, and population numbers while exhibiting colourful graphs and tables. Aliisa was only half listening. She was looking at the weird charts and equations on the PowerPoint, but not a lot of it made sense to her. Heck, she hadn't even talked to anyone but Ittuq and Anirniq for years, and Ani didn't even say anything back! Aliisa was just amazed that there were others still alive. She didn't care about this guy's facts and figures. *I can have my old life back.* Her thoughts started running away from her. She imagined everything being perfect, untouched, like nothing bad had ever happened. Some of her family and friends must have made it out alive like her. She'd be reunited with them straight away after the helicopter ride, they would jump back into normalcy, and they'd be happy again.

". . . so first the research team came up with a vaccine to prevent the infection in healthy individuals . . ."

She was making her own lists in her head, things she wanted to do when she got back to town. *I wonder if there are warm showers in Igloolik? What kind of food do they have at these centres we'll be in? I hope Doritos are still a thing. . . .*

". . . and then, surprisingly, they also found a medication to treat the infected. It envelops and stabilizes the virus in the infected cells, rendering the virus dormant. With continued treatment, we hope to completely eliminate the exposed cells from the body."

Wait, what? Aliisa started paying attention all of a sudden. Treating the infected? How could you turn a moving, rotten corpse back into a person?

"Greg himself," the doctor said, motioning to the helicopter pilot, "is in remission. He was exposed to the virus in northern Quebec. After we immobilized him, we successfully injected the treatment. So, he is able to perform normal duties, and he is once again a functioning member of society. Which is good for us at the centre because we are sorely in need of professionals like him. Normally he'd be in a quarantine centre, but exceptions have been made to those with in-demand skill sets. His treatment is injected twice daily. Actually, it's time for his morning dose. This will be good for you to see. It's quite simple really, nothing to worry about at all."

Aliisa looked at the pilot. *This guy is an ijiraujaq?* She cringed and wanted to reach for her rifle. But Greg just stood there as before, albeit a little sheepishly now that his status had been revealed. He did look pretty harmless. He wasn't attacking them, at least, or trying to bite her. He was wearing one of those blue work onesies qallunaat were so fond of. He was pretty nondescript, average height, plain qallunaaq face. The only special thing about this guy was that he was . . . dead? Or not dead. Somewhat dead? How do you describe someone who's being treated with medication to make them a living human again after being dead? *Do I say he* was *an ijiraujaq?* She side-eyed Greg, trying to figure out his humanhood.

Aliisa started out of her perplexity with the most important question of all: "Wait, doctor? You're saying you can turn ijiraujat—I mean, zombies—back into regular people? My whole family was turned into them before I left. Do you know if they're okay? Are they people again?" She waited with bated breath.

The doctor was messing around with his instruments. He had taken a set of vials from the cooler. "It's very possible. I don't know specifically right now. There are still a lot of unidentified patients to deal with. I wish I could tell you more, but even I don't have any sort of master list.

"Hmm," he muttered, switching his attention back to his supplies. He was rifling through the vials in the cooler, some of which had small films of ice on the outside of the glass. He selected an unfrozen vial, lifted it to eye level and peered in, shaking it slightly. "It's not usually clear like that." He noticed a separation near the surface of the contents and swirled the vial gently. "There we are," he said as the fluid mixed and became milky. He unwrapped a syringe and drew fluid into the barrel.

Greg had unzipped his navy-blue flight suit and rolled up the sleeve of the T-shirt underneath. Dr. English swabbed a section of waiting skin and expertly plunged the needle's shaft into Greg's arm.

"Done!" he smiled triumphantly. "Another patient in the clear." Greg just put his arm back into his suit, not really looking directly at either of them. Something told Aliisa that he wasn't as proud of his illness as the doctor was.

"Well, um. I suppose that's all. We should get your things packed up. I'm sorry, but we have a tight schedule. We can fly only during daylight hours, and we have a lot of ground to sweep today. We'll need to drop you off first to make room in the chopper; that'll eat up a lot of our search time. Oh, and your names! How many of you are there? I thought I saw a child over by the tent earlier. I should record your names now."

"I'm Aliisa, and there's a five-year-old boy we call Anirniq," Aliisa told him.

The doctor wrote down an approximation of the two children's names on his notepad and turned to direct his attention to Ittuq. "I'm going to have to report you and fill out a form of noncompliance if you refuse to come with us. The proper authorities will be sent. I mean, we're short on resources, but I'm no police officer! I'm not going to forcibly take you, but the children might be another story. Are you their grandfather?" he asked Ittuq.

Ittuq was absolutely fuming. "Not by blood," he mustered.

"Well, if you're not their official guardian, I'm authorized to remove the children from your care," proclaimed the doctor.

"Ah . . . uh . . . " said Aliisa. She was lost for words. She and Anirniq had both relied on Ittuq like a father. He had saved their lives countless times. He'd somehow gotten them out of populated areas when the outbreak was bad. He had shot hundreds of ijiraujaat. He was the one who had the skills to keep them safe from the ijiraujat, the wild animals, the elements. Aliisa hadn't known how to shoot, hunt, or camp. Actually, she hadn't known how to do much back then. She had never tried to convince him of anything—he was in charge; he knew everything; he could *do* anything. He took care of them like they were his own.

But . . . her family might be alive. Her friends, regular life—they still existed! Aliisa wanted to be warm and watch TV, drink hot chocolate again, and have friends. She felt *alone* out here. Since they'd left Iqaluit, she'd had no clue about the outside world. *Better than being dead,* she reminded herself. But she had to go back to town. She needed to find out who was still alive . . . or alive again.

Aliisa looked to Ittuq and said, "I don't want to go without you. Will you come too? Please?"

He switched to Inuktitut. "Aliisa, *aakuluk*, dear, you don't know if he's telling the truth. You can't trust this man. I know, I've been taken from the land before. They took me from my parents to go to residential school. They told us we'd be better off, we'd be fed, and have safe places to live. It didn't work out like that. They tried to kill our language, our culture. We were barely regarded as people. He's telling you you're going to a treatment centre for quarantine. You're going to be moved around like an animal and jailed until they say you can leave. I can't do that. I want you to think hard about this. You're old enough to make your own decisions, but really think about it. You have enough here, you have freedom. We have a happy life."

Aliisa looked at Ittuq, looked to the tent, to the lines with fish.

"Dr. English," she said, switching back to English, "how bad can a person get? I mean, can they come back if they're really far gone? Rotten and stuff?"

"There's no way of me knowing out here what happened to specific people, my dear. Someone will enter you into the database when we arrive at the regional centre and you can ask them all your questions. Anyway, we really do need to get on with this." He had lost interest while the two Inuit were conversing and looked anxious to go. "Why don't you go pack your things and say goodbye to mister, uh, this gentleman here," he said, gesturing to Ittuq. He didn't wait to hear anything else from her before he started bringing his equipment back to the helicopter.

"Uh, okay," she said to the doctor's back. She shuffled uncomfortably. "I'm sorry, Ittuq. I have to go and find out if my family is back. I miss them. I miss my old life." He looked like she had just smashed his heart into pieces. She couldn't look at him anymore. She stared at the ground and repeated, "I'm sorry."

She glanced up at him and quickly turned away, unable to meet his gaze. She went into the tent and looked around. Anirniq, looking terrified, was sitting in the middle of the sleeping skins. She surveyed their belongings: some tools for living on the land, some winter clothes, and a *qulliq*, a seal oil lamp. She didn't really need any of this stuff if she was going to live inside again. Everything looked smaller and older now. Her eyes had adjusted to the shiny technology and cleanness of the qallunaat already. She put a few little toys that Ittuq had made for Ani into her pocket, took Ani's hand, and exited the tent.

Aliisa felt terrible as she walked over to the waiting pilot. She was completely torn. This was all she'd known for three years. Sure, she had dreamed of going back, but now it felt different. She was flying into the unknown with two strange qallunaat and leaving Ittuq behind to live by himself. Her doubts about the situation flared. Maybe Ittuq was right. They didn't have it so bad out here, but . . . *My real family*, she thought. *I have to find out if they're back.* Ani had buried his face in Aliisa's snow pants. He peered out from under his hood at the strange pilot. Greg had an odd expression on his face and was positively leering at them. *Gross*, she thought as she looked away.

The doctor finished stowing his equipment, closed the back compartment of the helicopter, and held the passenger doors open to let Aliisa and Anirniq into the second row of seating.

"You're not going to need that," he said, gesturing to the rifle still slung across her back.

"Seriously?" Aliisa said, incredulously. "I've been carrying this every day for three years. This is why I'm still alive."

"This is a government mission. You need to be certified to carry a firearm. And besides, you're how old?"

"Thirteen," she said quietly.

"Ha! We have two adults here who are capable of taking care of you. You'll be fine without it from now on."

Aliisa definitely did not like this. But the doctor just stood there with his hand outstretched, waiting for her rifle. She took it off unwillingly and handed it to him. It felt strange to give up what had been her lifeline. The doctor set the rifle down on the ground.

"We have firearms and munitions stored properly in the back compartment. Honestly," he chuckled. "A thirteen-year-old with a firearm," she heard him mutter. He buckled them into their seats, pulled two pairs of headphones down from the ceiling, clamped them onto both of their heads and closed the door.

Aliisa was in shock. She felt completely powerless. Where was Ittuq? They hadn't even said goodbye. He had disappeared at some point; when? Was saying goodbye too hard? An empty hole opened up inside her. She held Ani's hand. She stared listlessly out at her now former home through the windows of this flying bubble. Ittuq was in the distance looking away. Her eyes started to water, looking at Ittuq alone out there. Now that she was really leaving, she started to panic. Maybe Ittuq was right, why is she trusting these strangers? Greg looked back at her and Ani. There was something wrong with this guy—his eyes had an unfocused glaze to them.

"I don't want to go," Aliisa said abruptly.

"You are coming with me to safety, child," said the doctor. "You two have your whole lives ahead of you. It's an utter waste out here in the middle of this frozen land. That old man can choose to die out here, but you're young, you need to be back in school like normal kids."

Aliisa choked down a sob. "I don't want to go!" she yelled. But Greg had already started the engine, and it drowned out most of her yelling, the rest coming through the audio equipment in loud bursts. The doctor flicked a button down and her microphone went silent. The rotors started to speed up above them, growing into a blur of movement. Aliisa struggled to catch her breath, sniffled, and wiped her eyes and nose with her sleeve. The helicopter grew weightless, the ground moving quickly beneath them as they shot forward into the sky. All of a sudden, the camp was gone. Ittuq was left behind. Ani was crying soundlessly, his microphone askew in front of his face. Aliisa squeezed his little hand. *What have I done?* she thought.

They flew west over the cold seawater, toward the mainland on the other side. They were high up out of the mist now. The sun was low in the sky and cut through the fog at their higher altitude. Aliisa watched Greg move the controls of the helicopter. She felt utterly helpless. Only a few hours ago, she hadn't thought her life would completely change. She squeezed more tears out of her eyes. She missed Ittuq; he had always listened to her. He didn't treat her like a child. She shouldn't have left!

The water went by under them, impervious to being abandoned.

The doctor had been huffily rooting around in his equipment. He handed Greg a Kleenex. For some reason, Greg had drool dripping down his face onto his flight suit. Aliisa realized she could hear them over the headphones. She found the control and turned up the audio.

". . . never seen this side effect before. Very odd. It must be this stupid climate," said the doctor. She could see him writing notes in his field pad. Greg was trying to slop up the drool with one hand, the other hand on the helicopter's joystick.

He had barely cleaned up his chin when the helicopter jerked backwards, hard. They were flung forward. Aliisa hit her head on the seat in front of her and her headphones fell off. The noise from the helicopter was loud in her ears now, but she could hear the doctor yelling at Greg. He was reaching over from the passenger seat, trying to grab the controls of the helicopter. Greg's whole body was stiff. He whipped his head from side to side, drool flinging onto the window and into the doctor's face. She watched him convulse again, hitting the joystick with his knee hard to the left. The helicopter slammed sideways. They hung from their seatbelts, the sea directly under them to the left.

Aliisa looked up at Ani hanging above her. He was trying to reach her, belted into his seat, face red with tears. In the front seat, Greg was snapping his mouth open and closed, straining at his seatbelt, his eyes wild and bulging. It looked like the doctor had been knocked unconscious. His head lolled around, his arms limp. The helicopter began to spin. The rotor was completely sideways, force-driving them around in circles rather than up. Greg's hands scrabbled as far as he could get them, trying desperately to get a hold of fresh meat; the controls were completely forgotten.

They swirled rapidly, falling fast, trapped together with the ijiraujaq. The icy cold sea shot upward at them at an incredible speed.

"Noooooo!!" Aliisa cried at no one in particular. She tried to grab Ani's hand, but she was glued in place by centrifugal force. Then there was a loud SMASH, a flash of light, and everything went black.

Sila

K.C. Carthew

Drastic changes in climate are evident by the appearances
of animal species that have never before been seen in the
Northwest Territories roaming throughout its various
regions. In recent years, mountain lions have been spotted
at the Arctic Circle. While some animals venture farther
north, others head south. . . .

STRINGS OF CHRISTMAS LIGHTS LINGER ALONG WINDOWS AND
brighten the neighbourhood as the daylight fades. Laila nurses her
baby girl, Sweetie Pie, in front of the living room window in the
warm comfort of the home she shares with her husband, Jimmy.
Sweetie Pie is ten months old. Constant joy and constant work.

They watch snowmobiles race across the frozen lake outside.
Laila's happy place is there, on the other side of the window.
Growing up in the Northwest Territories, it used to feel like winter
would last forever. But now, it's February and a balmy -3°C. Soon
they'll close the ice roads, and the time to walk on water will be over.

Sweetie Pie cries and Laila scans the room for a bright orange pacifier that she slips into Sweetie Pie's mouth, immediately calming her.

A 4Runner pulls up outside. Moments later, Jimmy appears indoors. He kisses Laila and playfully removes the pacifier from Sweetie Pie's mouth. Sweetie Pie starts to cry. *Pop!* The pacifier goes back in.

Laila grins. "Looks good for fishing!"

Jimmy appears less sure. Laila pokes him. "Scared I'll catch more fish?

Jimmy tickles her, mindful of Sweetie Pie. "No chance! Let's do it!"

Laila rubs her nose against Sweetie Pie's forehead. "Ready for your first ice-fishing trip?" She looks to Jimmy with pride. "I'm so excited to take her!" Jimmy nods. Nice to have a family and re-experience all the firsts. Life is good.

In the morning, Jimmy checks the outside thermometer. It's -7°C. "You're right. Great day for fishing!" He heads outside while Laila puts on her winter gear. She places Sweetie Pie carefully in the pouch of her *amauti*. Before leaving, Laila removes a rifle case from the hallway closet and pockets a box of bullets.

Outside, Jimmy tops up the snowmobile with gasoline, then inspects a small towing sled that includes another gas can, anti-freeze, firewood, fishing rods, an ice auger, a cooler, a thermos, and blankets. Ready. As Laila sits on the snowmobile with Sweetie Pie snug and safe in the amauti, the orange pacifier falls to the ground. "Ha! Don't want to forget this!" Jimmy picks it up, wipes it off, and tucks it in his coat pocket. "Ready to rock?"

Laila grins. "Always." She squeezes his shoulder, and away they go, rocketing across the lake and into the bush.

It's lake after lake and then back into the bushes, where the going is slower as they navigate around clusters of thin spruce trees. Finally, they burst onto another lake. What a glorious day. Laila basks in the sunshine as she closes her eyes and presses into Jimmy's back.

When her eyes flicker open, she spots movement along the shore and signals to Jimmy, who slows down as they approach a flipped snowmobile. A young man in his twenties stumbles along the ice. He appears weak and tired. Jimmy calls out to him, and the man turns quickly and falls. Jimmy jumps off the snowmobile and rushes to help him. Laila unpacks the thermos from the sled. The man seems dizzy and disoriented. His gloves are missing. Laila finds them in the snow. She grabs a blanket from the sled and wraps it around the man. His lips are blue. "We've got to get him to the hospital." Jimmy agrees and tries to upright the man's snowmobile. The engine turns, but the tread is torn, which means the snowmobile is not going anywhere.

Laila removes the items from the sled so that Jimmy can lay the man on it. She gets back on the snowmobile. Jimmy pushes the throttle to its limit, but there isn't enough power to tow everyone. Laila dismounts. "I'll stay with Sweetie Pie and set up. It should take you an hour, an hour and a half to get to town and back?"

Jimmy nods and gestures to Sweetie Pie. "Is she still sleeping?"

Laila checks. "She's out. Must be our lucky day!"

Jimmy grins. "Okay, I'll be back as soon as I can." He looks to Sweetie Pie. "Take care of your mom."

Ha! As if Laila needs help; she was raised in the bush. She surveys the surroundings: thin trees and rock demarcate the landscape behind her. Everything else is snow and ice as far as the eye can see. She gets to work, using a small axe to hack branches from a balsam fir tree that she places around the firewood she unpacked from one of the crates that was on the sled. As she lights the fire, she feels movement in the amauti, and a few small whimpers reach her ears. She sits and pulls Sweetie Pie forward to breastfeed, humming and smiling. Despite the setback, it remains a beautiful day.

Laila augers a hole in the ice. She dunks her line in and within seconds, catches a fish. Its tail flaps, but quickly stiffens, already starting to freeze in the cold. Ecstatic, Laila removes Sweetie Pie from the amauti to show her the fish and let her touch its scaly skin. "That's a jackfish!" Laila says, and Sweetie Pie's eyes brighten.

Movement in the distance catches her eye. Laila places the jackfish in the cooler and picks up Sweetie Pie, staring at the horizon. The shape in the distance is significant, but she can't make it out yet. Whatever it is seems to be approaching fast. "What the hell?" she mutters. "Is that a bear?" She looks nervously at Sweetie Pie and puts her back in the amauti. Instinct tells her to load the rifle. She fires into the air. Sweetie Pie cries. The shot is loud and threatening, and she expects the animal to retreat. Instead, whatever it is continues to swagger towards them.

Laila loads another bullet and fires. The rifle jams. It's cold—no surprise. Laila immediately pours antifreeze over the action and lays the rifle across the extra balsam fir branches next to the fire to warm it up. She dumps out the box of bullets and counts. Three bullets left—four, including the one that's jammed.

Sweetie Pie is still crying. "Shh! It's okay," Laila soothes. She searches her pockets. It dawns on her that Jimmy has the pacifier. *Fuck.* She swings the amauti around and offers Sweetie Pie her finger to suck on. Sweetie Pie calms down. Laila squints at the approaching figure and instantly realizes she needs her finger back. A polar bear is heading towards them. *How is that possible?* she thinks frantically. *What is a polar bear doing this far south?*

The rifle thaws and fires. Laila quickly reloads.

She looks to the boulders that come up from the water's edge and spots an overhang at the top that might have a small cave they can hide in.

With Sweetie Pie in the amauti, the rifle in one hand, and the axe in the other, Laila moves swiftly through the snow.

From below, the way up the rocks is not obvious. Sweetie Pie makes noises. "It's okay, my girl," Laila says, trying to keep her voice steady. She starts to climb. Her heart pounds. She wills her hands to stop shaking. They do.

The polar bear approaches the defunct snowmobile.

Laila continues to climb. She looks over her shoulder. The polar bear stands and sniffs the air. Even at this distance, Laila can see its ribs. She holds still against the rock.

The polar bear passes by the fire, sniffing along the ground until it reaches the cooler. Within seconds, it rips the cooler open and swallows the jackfish. While the bear is distracted, Laila climbs. Her breath is heavy. She reasserts her grip and hoists herself onto the ledge at the top of the small cliff.

Sweetie Pie makes unhappy noises. Laila sets the axe down and swings the amauti around, cuddling Sweetie Pie to her chest. Keeping her right hand on the rifle, Laila removes her left glove and urges Sweetie Pie to suckle her finger. "Good girl," Laila whispers. "We're okay."

But they aren't.

A small cave to the side of the ledge has an opening wide enough for her to fit. Laila crawls into it. Light from outside barely fills the space, which is only a few feet deep.

Laila removes her amauti and creates a cradle for Sweetie Pie. She shivers. Her breath lingers thick in the air in front of her.

She peers outside and watches the polar bear sniff the snow, moving slowly away from the weakening flame of the fire toward the rocky incline. Clearly, the bear can sense their presence; it just can't quite figure out exactly where they are—yet.

Laila lines up the rifle. She has a good shot from the mouth of the cave and takes it. She hits—but just barely. It's not enough. The polar bear roars. Two bullets remain.

Sweetie Pie shrieks. "Sh!" Laila hushes, this time unable to keep the panic out of her voice. Laila plugs her finger into Sweetie Pie's mouth and kisses her face. "It's okay, my girl, it's okay. Mama loves you."

Glancing back outside, Laila realizes she has lost sight of the polar bear. It's on to them. In fact, it's under them, desperately contemplating how to climb up to the ledge. Laila removes her finger from Sweetie Pie's mouth to reload.

Sweetie Pie whimpers. "No!" Laila hisses. "Sh!" She tucks the amauti more snugly around Sweetie Pie and places her farther back in the cave before creeping slowly out toward the ledge. Laila's hands tremble. "Stop!" she whispers harshly, but they tremble anyway. She glances over the ledge. The bear is two metres below. On impulse, she picks up the axe and whips it at the bear. The axe glances off the animal's shoulder, and it winces and growls in anger. Hurling itself upward, it leaps at her, coming within a foot of the ledge.

Laila reels back, but stands her ground, moving backwards to position the rifle between the edge, where the bear will appear, and the mouth of the cave. The heavy chuffing of the polar bear causes her heart to pound harder. Sweetie Pie screams. Laila keeps both hands on the rifle.

Suddenly, the polar bear is on the ledge. Laila fires. She hits its paw. It's not enough. One bullet left.

The polar bear snarls, its breath heavy and excited, heading directly for Laila. Sweetie Pie instinctively becomes quiet. Laila looks at her and starts to melt. She shakes it off, wipes her eyes, and exhales deeply.

Laila aims at the bear, knowing the odds of stopping it with a single bullet.

She aims into the cave. Sweetie Pie looks confused and scared.

Laila looks back and forth in desperation between the beast and her baby.

"Mama loves you," she whispers.

Laila fires.

The Wildest Game

Jay Bulckaert

MY PRUNE,

If you're reading this, then the jig is up, as they say. I felt the need to put this down in writing in case I'm not available to explain myself. I know what I've done is horrifying to everyone, but especially to you. Believe me, even I had a period of time when I couldn't believe what I was doing. I have actively caused harm, and although I do regret the fallout of my actions on the family of the person in question, I don't believe what I did was technically wrong. I know you'll hate that, but there's no point in being anything less than totally honest now. We are all animals, part of an ecosystem, and when one group in nature overpopulates, the food chain has a way of naturally culling the rampant species. When rabbit numbers go up, so do lynx numbers. It's a perfect balance. Except with humans. Somewhere along the line we misunderstood our place here; we created a way to beat Mother Earth's natural balancing act, the give and take that keeps everything in symbiotic order. I tried to find a way to heal myself, and although I know you won't think so, part of this was meant help the world out a bit. Just so it's said, you were never going to be one of my harvests, and despite what you think of me now, I do love you. Anyways, I hope this helps explain things a little bit.

It took a bit of research to get the right combination of things. The main priority was to find a place that had considerably less pollution. Air and water needed to have consistently below national averages. I studied each province and territory for a year before I made the call to head north to Yellowknife. It wasn't just the air and water, though—it also came down to four other factors that would ensure the longevity of my lifestyle. On my list were the following items in no real order:

- Must be remote; generally cut off from a larger, more skilled police presence
- Easy access to hunting and hunting culture as a guise for the meat culled
- Fit and active residents
- Temperatures some of the coldest in the country year-round

I guess I've been a cannibal my whole life. I've been chewing at my fingers and cuticles since I can remember. (I know you hated that and would always try to get me to stop.) The other day I tried to calculate how much of my own skin I've ingested in the past forty years, and I figured that I probably ate a pound of it each year. I chew on them incessantly every day. I've literally eaten a fifth of my body weight in my own flesh. It adds up over the years.

My buddy made the joke once that it looked like I dipped my fingers into a paper shredder. It was funny at the time, something I just laughed off, but it's an image I've never been able to get out of my mind: two hands slowly rising up out of the gory, whirring blades, fingertips mangled, red, and dripping. So I suppose that the leap to eating other human flesh wasn't that much of a stretch for me. I already knew the taste of my own skin intimately and had started to prefer it more than other kinds of meat. Gradually, I stopped eating store-bought meat almost altogether. There was a gaminess to the taste that I couldn't shake; even chicken started to taste off every time I had it. One night while cooking, I cut a sizable chunk off my thumb—you know the one, you'd kiss the scar some- times when we were watching TV together? What I didn't tell you about that scar was that it only took a few minutes of consideration while I stood there, draining my thumb over the sink and staring at the chunk of fingertip lying next to a carrot, to fry it up. I had considered using some sea salt, coarse pepper, and crushed garlic but at the last moment decided to eat it pure, without seasoning. I'll never forget that first morsel of my own flesh: not surface skin anymore but dense flesh, dark and purple, deeply rich and velvety.

The real seeds of this obsession were planted back when I was living in Toronto, working that job in advertising I told you I hated. I was overweight, tired all the time, stressed out and depressed. The usual city grind. I couldn't help but feel like I was caught in this oppressive fog of noise, pollution, and unhealthy humans. The summers were becoming unbearable with the ever-rising heat and humidity, and I couldn't think straight anymore. I felt like it was steaming my brain, cooking me from the inside out, and that feeling bled into everything else. I felt unhealthy at my core, and everything in my life started to take on a grimy, suffocating dimness. Everything was pre-packaged down south, from my food to my conversations. A life made in a factory and sealed in plastic.

My company was doing a PR job for a high-end Wagyu beef outfit, and that's what started this whole thing. The cattle are treated like humans. They are spoken to kindly every day, they get massages, and when the time comes, they are harvested in low numbers so the other cattle around them aren't aware anyone is missing. The meat then has -43°C air blown over it to put it into a state of "hibernation," which greatly enhances the quality of the meat. I spoke to celebrities and athletes, academics and well-to-do health nuts who all praised the nutritional properties of ingesting meat like this. Many talked about how it changed their lives.

This is what triggered my interest in cannibalism and the life-changing properties to be found in ingesting well-preserved human flesh. If the best beef in the world is that way because it was treated like a healthy human, I wondered how much better human meat might be if its owner treated themselves as well as those cattle. So I looked up the coldest cities in Canada, cities that weren't so small a missing person would be instantly detected, but remote enough to allow for ample hunting grounds and areas to dispose of bodies where they'd never be found. Yellowknife, it turns out, is on the shore of Great Slave Lake, which is the deepest lake in North America, and that was the final deciding factor. Gut piles and bones and DNA in general would be hard to find at 2,000 feet deep.

Yellowknife was cold as a bastard. Remember last year when we had a two-week stretch where it was technically colder here than it was on Mars? The cold took a little getting used to. I settled into my new job. Making friends was easy. It's true what you'd tell me about Northern hospitality: the weather is cold, but the hearts are warm. I got introduced to ice fishing, dog sledding, whiskey-drowned Scrabble nights in a shack, two-stepping at the Range, and those jaw-dropping northern lights. It's not even worth trying to describe their insane beauty on paper, I'm sure you'd agree.

Soon enough I had a group of friends, had moved up at my job, and we had just started dating. Life was good. But I figured it was time to tackle the reason I had come north in the first place. The first order of business was to learn to hunt. Remember all the weekends I'd be gone with Barry and come back with near-death stories? Well, part of doing that was to get myself used to the act of killing and to learn how to butcher a large animal. Part of that was to build up the expectation that it would be normal for me to have large cuts of meat in my freezer, that when I came back from a weekend away with some blood on my hunting gear, it was just another successful hunting trip. Part of it was to convince you, specifically, that all of this would be normal from there on in (I'm sorry for the deception). So I spent those first two years inviting myself on every hunting trip I could. I learned to track animals, look for their habitats and where they feed. But what I really learned was patience and prediction. Understanding the nature of an animal and how it would behave, how to hide and be still so it would nearly offer itself to me. And I learned that I had no problem with the gore of it all.

This is something I never told you about because I knew you'd find it disturbing: I remember Barry shooting the first moose I had ever seen. A cow down by the water with her calf. Barry took a 200-yard shot. She shivered suddenly, took three steps, and dropped into the knee-high water, flailing around. I remember thinking that I should feel bad for the calf standing there watching its mom drown, face down, but I didn't. I didn't feel cruelty though, I just felt nothing. A warm, black void is the only way I can describe it. When Barry cut her gut open, he nicked her teats, and I remember watching with childlike amusement the stream of milk mix into the blood, creating an inky swirl of pink. It reminded me of that gross strawberry milk I'd sometimes drink as a kid. A year later when I shot my own moose for the first time, it confirmed everything I had suspected. I had no problem killing something. The massive beast stood there, about twenty feet from me. We had called it in towards us. I remember being scared and nervous, but once it stood there in front of me, offering itself up, my world went quiet and that dark, warm void washed over me. I calmly aimed the .300 just behind its front quarter and pulled the trigger. That moose dropped like it was suddenly just unplugged from a wall, dead before it hit the ground. It's amazing once you learn how to clean an animal, it's almost like they were made to be taken apart piece by piece.

Humans are no different. Their legs come off pretty easily once you hit the right tendon in the ball joint of the hip. No different than a moose, really. Once you hear that telltale "pop," the leg is off. Much like a moose, you don't take much from the knee down. Calf muscles are pretty sinewy, and the thigh muscle—especially inner thigh—would make for the most tender of roasts. Arms are similar. A lot less meat than the legs, obviously, but they'd be great for stews. My favourite cut was the backstrap, right along the spine on the inside, so you'd have to gut them first, split the rib cage open then reach into that gory cavity and carve down each side of the spine. It's not much meat, but it is the most tender, rich, and revitalizing meat that exists. There truly is nothing else like it.

I decided early on to only take males, just so it's said. I find the idea of killing women abhorrent. Truthfully, I don't really enjoy killing in the first place, it's just that I also don't feel anything about it either. And it's much easier to kill a man than a woman. It's easy to look inside yourself as a fellow man and see all those dark secrets, horrible thoughts, moronic attitudes, and then take your self-hatred out on some poor bastard who you know harbours all the same flaws deep down. All men are the same, some are just better at hiding this shared disease than others.

I carefully considered my first harvest in every respect. I became fast friends with Stanley from the first time I met him, as you'll remember. He'd been trapping since he was thirteen, just stopped going to school as a kid and would set rabbit snares in his backyard. That he allowed me to run his trapline with him last winter just seemed like it was meant to be. One of the reasons I chose Stanley was because from a young age, he had been eating only country food. Moose, pike fresh from the river, lynx, ptarmigan, beaver, and bear. I watched him closely over that winter to see what his habits were, and he lived clean. The occasional beer here and there, but otherwise no junk food, nothing processed. He spent his entire winter outside in -35°C temperatures. It stood to reason that his flesh would be pure, pristine, and chilled.

Mentally, he was fit, too. Unlike me, he didn't suffer from rage or depression. He was even-keel all the time, and that mattered a lot to me. I had initially wanted someone who meditated as well because I believe that a person's mental well-being affects the chemical composition of their flesh. As my acupuncturist says, "If you don't deal with an issue, it ends up in your tissue." But I learned that running that trapline was his form of meditation, and he did that six hours a day for nine months straight. Stanley was my friend, and he was also the perfect harvest.

I'm sure by now you've figured out that Stanley wasn't eaten by wolves last February when I was running his trapline with him. I'm sorry for lying to you and for all the consoling you did that I had to pretend I needed. It was easy to convince the RCMP at the time because everyone knew the risks he took by living in the bush. Running a trapline is a dangerous business. It goes with the territory. It's part of the risk every trapper assumes. Sort of a "live by the bush, die by the bush" resolution.

For what it's worth, I did my best to make his death as painless and quick as possible. He was my friend, after all. I know how that sounds, but it's still true. I simply shot him behind the ear with a .17 HMR round, just like I'd seen him do to countless animals. He was checking a conibear trap that had a wolverine in it. The thing was snarling and still alive. It had chewed halfway through its own leg trying to free itself. Stanley was about to dispatch it, and I had to act quickly.

Once Stanley had stopped spasming, I quickly set about taking a leg and an arm, part of a buttock, and one backstrap. I wanted to leave enough of Stanley so the scene would look right. At one point, I looked up and the wolverine had stopped snarling. It was sitting there, silently watching me dissect my friend. We had this strange moment together, not scared or disapproving, just one predator acknowledging another.

Once I had the meat packed up, I approached the wolverine to knock it out. It went berserk, shearing a crater in the snow, trying to escape and attack all at once. I managed to whack it with the butt of the gun hard enough to stun it, and then delivered two more blows to knock it out cold. I gently released the catch of the trap and pried it open just enough that the wolverine could free itself when it came to.

Sitting at a safe distance thirty minutes later, I watched as the animal jolted back to life, angry as hell. It wrenched its bloody paw free of the trap and stood there for a minute, surprised, before noticing Stanley lying right in front of it, half dissected. Within ten minutes, it had torn a hole in Stanley's guts and eaten half of his intestines. It gnawed at the raw leg and arm stumps I had left, perfectly replacing my incision marks with savagely torn flesh. It even ate most of Stanley's face, concealing the tiny bullet hole behind his ear under a bloody, pulpy mess. I wasn't worried about the police finding the round in the autopsy. There's a reason assassins use calibre that size for their hits: the round shatters and, at the very least, becomes untraceable.

I won't go into much more detail, but I will say that eating Stanley made me feel alive in a way I never have. I know that's hard for you to hear. I hibernated his flesh in an old meat cache Stanley had set up. It never got to -43°C out there, but the -35°C temperatures still did wonders. I felt clean inside—not just inside my guts, but inside my mind and my soul. I felt clear and precise. I felt extremely efficient and powerful. I felt optimized. I sat in that cabin alone for a week eating every morsel, and by the end, I felt new.

By the time the RCMP arrived on the scene, a pack of wolves had been through and apparently all that was left was Stanley's lower jaw. The evidence was gone. My alibi was that I simply had stayed behind that day due to a cold and he ran the line solo, like he usually did anyways. It was simple and easy. In the end, it's probably for the best that I completely forgot about Stanley's trail camera in the midst of the chaos. I guess when I went to knock that ol' wolverine out, it kicked a bunch of snow against the camera, hiding it from my view. Last week when the police went back to do a final sweep now that the snow has melted, they saw the camera that had remained hidden in the winter. Everything was perfectly recorded.

Like I say, it's probably best they found it, because I don't think I would have stopped, to be honest. I'm sure you're completely disgusted by this stage, and I understand. You have the right. But I did feel the need to be truthful and say that I'm sorry. The RCMP have surrounded the house. We are in hour three of a standoff now (I told them I have hostages in here), but I've kept them at bay long enough to write this and have one last sip of that good whiskey we got from your brother last Christmas. This won't hurt.

Love you more,
JB

Strays

Repo Kempt

DR. LYKKE JEPSEN PULLED THE EXPOSED LIVER TO ONE SIDE with a gloved finger. *Where the hell is the bleed*, she asked herself. A gust of wind hammered the building, causing the cheap floodlights surrounding her to flicker. The aging portable heater sputtered and faltered before revving up again. Outside, a blizzard had descended on the hamlet of Kinngait—barely more than a thousand people nestled in a frozen inlet on the lowest corner of Baffin Island. The veterinary technician, Margo, strained to keep the dog's ribs spread open with both hands while keeping a watchful eye on the anesthesia machine. Her arms trembled with fatigue, sending faint shudders through the makeshift operating table.

"Hold it steady," barked Lykke. If only they'd brought the stainless-steel spreaders from their clinic—one of the many luxuries she missed when travelling across the Arctic. None of the smaller communities had the means to afford or maintain a veterinary clinic, so the government flew up professionals twice a year to deal with anything that didn't require dogs to be sent south for major operations.

"Fucking hell," she mumbled. "It has to be here somewhere." Lykke sopped up the excess blood in the cavity with a sterile sponge, dropping it at her side before grabbing another. Dozens of crimson swabs littered the area around her feet after a long day of operations.

A cough sounded from behind her. She had forgotten the observers. Edna, the owner of the hotel, an elderly woman with a thick Polish accent, and Markoosie, a local Inuit hunter in his 50s who had brought the dog in. They would have been finished for the day if it wasn't for the accident. He said he would've put it out of its misery with his rifle after it ran into the path of his snowmobile, but it belonged to a local elder. Knowing how much the dog meant to the old woman, he had driven it to the clinic in hopes of saving it.

"I can't find the damn bleed," said Lykke, throwing another blood-soaked sponge to the floor in frustration. Hopes of stabilizing the dog and sending it to a proper veterinary clinic in the south were fading fast. *Snick-snick-snick.* An irritating sound jerked her attention to a cluttered corner of the filthy garage. Lykke squinted hard into the darkness beyond the cheap spotlights. Nothing but shadows and piles of junk. She'd heard it five times—or was it six—since they'd started surgeries that morning. Unable to find the source, Lykke focused back on the exposed organs of the dying dog.

"He's got an arrhythmia," said Margo, shifting her body position in an effort to give her tired arms a rest.

"Blood pressure?" asked Lykke without looking up from the animal's viscera.

"I don't know. The machine keeps resetting."

"Just look at his gums," said Lykke, with a frustrated huff. "Do they look pale?"

"Sorry," said Margo. "Yes, they're pale."

Despite the coldness of the room, the overhead surgical lights had Lykke sweating profusely. The pungent odour of dog feces from an earlier mishap tainted the stale air around the table. The lights flickered again, forcing Lykke to blink rapidly to regain her focus. Through the frosted window across the table, the hotel next door faded in and out of view like a ghost ship in the blowing snow. She brushed a stray hair out of her eyes with her sleeve to avoid getting blood on her face. It was bad form, she knew, but sterility protocols were more lax than normal given the conditions.

"We're low on iso," said Margo. "Gotta speed things up, or we're running out."

Lykke jammed more swabs into the dog's abdomen, desperate to find the torn vessel. The steady hissing and puffing of the blood pressure machine set her nerves on edge. The lights flickered again. A dull buzz from her cell phone droned incessantly in her pocket. Despite her best efforts to ignore it, her mind flashed to who might be calling. One thing she knew for certain—it wasn't Michael on the line.

"We better not lose power," said Margo.

Lykke ignored her, wishing she'd been able to find a more experienced technician to accompany her. Last-minute trips always left her scrambling to find an assistant. She pushed another sponge into the dog's abdomen to sop up the abundance of blood.

"His temp has dropped," said Margo. The probe attached to the monitor flashed the dog's internal temperature. "Thirty-four and falling."

"I found it," Lykke exclaimed, reaching over to the hemostats on the tray beside her while keeping a tight pinch on the artery in her fingers. She clamped off the bleeding vessel and leaned back to stretch the tightness in her lower back. "Let's get him sewn up."

She no sooner had the clamp in place when a loud crash erupted near the exit. Lykke turned to face it with her bloody gloves held at shoulder height. Markoosie lay sprawled out on his back with Edna crouching over him.

"I think he's having a heart attack," said Edna with a bewildered expression. She covered her mouth with both hands.

"Check his pulse," said Lykke, glancing back into the dog on the table to check that the clamp was holding.

"He's not breathing," shouted Edna through her fingers. "He's not even breathing!"

Lykke flashed an anguished look at Margo before tearing off her gloves and rushing to the fallen man. She shouldered Edna out of the way and knelt to check for vital signs. No heartbeat, no respiration. She struggled to unzip Markoosie's parka before pumping on his chest in steady compressions. Margo stood still, looking helpless. Her eyes pleaded for instruction from her superior.

After a series of compressions, Lykke shouted to Margo: "Grab the AED machine from the hotel wall."

Margo hesitated, frozen in position. "But the dog," she cried, still clutching the animal's ribcage.

"Fuck the dog," said Lykke. "He's going to die. Get the machine. Now!"

Margo released the dog's ribs, and its yawning abdomen slid closed. She ripped off her surgical gloves and dashed past Lykke, leaping over the fallen hunter's legs on her way to the exit. Yanking the door open, Margo pulled on her parka as she crossed the threshold with Edna hobbling after her into the storm, shouting something about a key to the office. A gust of icy Arctic wind swirled into the room, sending snowflakes and dozens of discarded medical wrappers churning into the air. Lykke's bare arms erupted in gooseflesh. The door slammed against the inner wall behind her, triggering a stir in the slumbering dog. Lykke kept compressing in a steady rhythm while straining to shut it with her outstretched foot. At the edge of her reach, the door was still inches from her boot.

Lykke was focused on the hunter's flaccid expression when a low moan erupted from the tabletop. The animal convulsed on the table, thrashing violently against its restraints. *The isophlorane*, she thought. *It's run out.* In the rush of the emergency, they had neglected to secure the dog's front paws, leaving only the hind legs tied down. It squirmed and fell from the table, crashing onto the concrete. The intubation tube, which was taped to its snout, remained deep in its throat. Blood poured freely from its open abdomen, steaming as it splashed onto the cold, concrete floor. Its convulsions tore its hind legs loose from the straps and the dog staggered to its feet, bloody viscera drooping out from its gaping abdomen. Lykke and the confused animal locked eyes before it rushed toward her in sheer panic, dragging the tubes still connected to its body behind it, pulling down the IV pole and tearing the intubation tube from the ventilator. She tucked her head down and closed her eyes, bracing for the impact. But the dog leapt past her through the open door and out into the darkness of the storm.

Lykke slumped against the hallway wall outside her hotel room, chin against her chest. The fluorescent lights overhead flickered periodically as the blizzard wind pounded into the hotel with a steady rhythm. Margo stepped out of her room across the corridor holding a flask of cheap rye.

"What a night," said Margo, taking a swig of the liquor before sitting down beside her.

Lykke raised her head to accept the offer of a drink. "Total fucking madness."

Both women erupted in nervous laughter.

"I guess we better keep it down," said Lykke. "Don't wanna wake the neighbours."

"No stress," said Margo. "Edna said other guests flew out before the storm rolled in."

"Lucky them," said Lykke. "So we've got the place to ourselves then?"

Margo nodded, eyes closed, inhaling deeply, savouring the burn of the whiskey. "You saved that guy's life."

"We both did," said Lykke. "He wouldn't have lived without the AED, and I couldn't have kept him alive if you weren't there to get it."

Margo didn't acknowledge the comment. "I'm sorry I hesitated."

"Totally normal reaction. That guy was more important than the dog."

"I don't think I'll ever get used to seeing them die," said Margo, frowning at the thought.

A wave of disappointment washed over Lykke. *She's not going to last long at this game.* "You'd better get used to it. I've lost hundreds of dogs over the years."

"Do you ever feel bad about it?"

"Sure. But death is a part of this job. You just get used to it."

Lykke's phone buzzed in her pocket and she struggled to pull it out. Cell service was spotty in most Arctic towns. Three missed calls, one voicemail. Her mother-in-law twice and another number she didn't recognize. She clicked off the screen and stuffed it back in. Her thoughts drifted to Michael. Six weeks ago, he'd told her he'd been seeing someone, that he wanted a divorce. Lykke had smashed a vase against the living room wall, insults had been exchanged. He'd stormed out, telling her he was driving out to the cabin to clear his head. He never came home.

Margo lowered her eyes, sadness seeping into her features. "Any word on whether or not they found him?"

Lykke tried to answer, but the words caught in her throat. She eyed Margo with a puzzled expression before realizing that she was talking about the escaped dog rather than her husband.

Lykke offered Margo a weak smile. "Edna asked a couple of locals to check around the area. He can't have survived long in that shape. Especially with the weather."

"But he couldn't have gotten far."

"He might have curled up under something. Animals do that. They hide to die. The blood trail would've been lost in the drifting snow." She thought of the dog slipping between the steel stilts of the building and curling up to die under the crawlspace. Her body tensed, imagining the dog writhing in agony as the anaesthetic wore off. Thoughts of Michael lingered underneath.

Margo nodded, pondering the whole ordeal before taking another drink.

"I can't believe it just ran out."

"Not the first dog I've had wake up under sedation," said Lykke. "I had one tear loose and try to bite me once. Nearly took my face off." She hauled a hearty swig of whiskey before replacing the cap. She had a momentary thought about whether she should be drinking given her medication but let the idea pass. *Fuck it, I've earned it after this day.*

"I can't believe it's only a week until we're headed home," said Margo.

Home. Lykke's heart sank at the word. The pair had been on the road for a month, travelling from town to town across the Arctic. A sudden wave of exhaustion swept over her at the thought of returning to her empty house, the depressing tones of her consoling friends, and the whirlwind of scenarios she might be required to face.

"I'm crashing," said Lykke, pushing herself to her feet. "I'll see you in the morning."

"I hope you sleep better than last night," said Margo. "You should try earplugs like me."

Lykke closed her eyes and stood, her legs unsteady from the drink and lack of blood flow. "I think I'll try Ambien instead."

Lykke shuffled across her hotel room and flopped onto the bed fully clothed. She pulled her T-shirt up over her head, laying it over her face to block out the ceiling light. The fabric smelled of sweat and chemical cleaner. When she shut her eyes, a vision of the dying Inuit man surfaced, clutching her arm when she revived him. His eyes wild, his expression crazed. The smell of his breath, sweet and rotten, hot on Lykke's face. Then the dog rushing toward her, blood streaming from its tender underbelly. Lykke sat up with a start and threw the shirt aside.

Her phone vibrated, and she scrambled to find it in the tangle of sheets. Another voicemail notification. She took two pills—a Gabapentin and a Paxil—and turned on the television using the remote, flicking aimlessly through all the channels several times before shutting it off. In the silence that followed, wind ripped around the building, causing the whole structure to shudder. The drone of a snowmobile rose and faded as it passed the front of the hotel. Curiosity got the better of her, and she tapped the voicemail icon and waited for the message.

"Lykke, it's Deb." Her mother-in-law's voice sounded weak and tired. "They found Michael's boat on the other side of the lake, but there's still no sign of him. I really hope you're okay up there. I know you're busy, but please, just call me back."

Lykke heard a faint sob as the woman ended the message. She tossed the phone back onto the bed beside her; the other messages could wait. Rolling onto one side, her lower back aching from the too-low surgical table, she flexed her fingers. Her joints were stiff and sore from working in the cold. Gases from the anaesthetic machine had seeped from the mouths of the sleeping canines all day, contaminating the air quality. The fumes had left her with a rumbling headache. She stripped off the rest of her clothes on her way to turn off the light and then crawled under the sheets.

Hours later, she awoke in a cold sweat, the sound of her own moans startling her back into the waking world. Flashes of her nightmare—the dog convulsing on the floor of the makeshift surgery suite, gutted wide open, an intubation tube dangling from his gaping mouth—faded into the darkness of the room. She considered turning on the light but abandoned the idea by the time her feet hit the floor. It wasn't until she reached the bathroom door that she remembered that Michael had been somewhere in the dream. An image of him flashed in Lykke's mind as she fished out a pill from her toiletry bag in the dark—his face underwater, sinking down into the murky depths of the lake. She recalled sitting in

Michael's boat with his inert body, stroking his hair as hard rain fell all around them. His eyes closed, an expression of disappointment. Even in death, he frowned upon everything she did. *You can take one more*, she told herself. *It will take more than three to overdose.* She crunched the pill between her teeth before washing it down with a glass of tap water and heading back to bed.

Lykke had slept like a dead woman: lying on her back, hands limp on her chest. She rolled over to look at the glowing red numbers of the bedside clock. It was twenty minutes before her alarm was set to go off. She remembered another dream, less frightening than the last. She'd been standing on the deck of the cabin in the autumn breeze, the leaves a sea of orange and red. There were dogs everywhere, hundreds of them, surrounding the shed and the outhouse, filling the dirt driveway leading to the front door, lining the beach near the dock. She knew, without fully understanding how, that they were all the dogs she'd ever let die on her table. They were all there: the dog from that morning, the cocker spaniel she'd lost in her first week at the clinic, her uncle's corgi, for whose death he'd never forgiven her. All of the canine eyes were fixed on her as she stood on the porch. Lykke remembered looking down and realizing that there was a large wolfhound chewing on her outstretched hand. There was no pain, but the hand was mangled beyond recognition. The white fur around the dog's snout was matted with blood. She rubbed her eyes hard to wipe the last remnants of dream from her mind.

She lay awake, her mouth arid, the taste of the rye still clinging to her tongue, wishing she hadn't given the flask back to Margo. Lykke rummaged through the twisted sheets on the bed to find her phone. One missed call, one new voicemail. She dialed the voice-mail function and waited for the message. "It's Trina. Police were here yesterday asking about drugs missing from the clinic. If you get this message, I need to talk with you asap."

Lykke hit delete and went to the washroom for a second time, taking another Ambien. This wasn't going to leave her alone. This wasn't going to go away. As she grabbed the edge of the sheet to crawl back into bed, she heard the same steady clicking from the surgery suite, moving back and forth outside the door. *Snick-snick-snick.*

Must be the radiators, she thought. *Air in the pipes.* She crept to the door, listening intently, but the sound had gone.

By dawn, the storm had subsided. An eerie calm had settled upon Kinngait. Lykke chipped away at the ice-encrusted padlock on the garage until she could insert her key. Once inside, she kept her winter clothes on until the portable heater warmed the room to the point that her breath was no longer visible. She checked the clinic schedule for the day. The list featured a dozen canines with a variety of ailments and required procedures—neuters, spays, lumpectomies, and dental cleanings. Lykke tried to wipe the remaining sleep from her eyes with her sleeve. The taste of vomit mingled with mint toothpaste in her mouth. Her stomach had decided to reject the energy bar and coffee she had eaten within minutes of wolfing them down. She popped two pieces gum out of their foil packaging and tossed them into her mouth.

"No sign of your fugitive," declared Edna between stomps of her boots on the threshold.

Lykke paused, staring at the floor where the dog had landed, before smiling to greet Edna.

The older woman removed her gloves and warmed her hands on the heater. "Markoosie is certainly glad you chose him over the dog."

Lykke laughed, albeit rather weakly. "Not a hard choice to make."

Margo appeared in the doorway behind Edna, pulling off her toque and mittens.

"Only minus twenty-nine this morning," said Margo.

"Practically balmy," said Lykke, and the pair set to preparing for the day's work.

Near mid-afternoon, between the sixth and seventh procedures, Lykke heard the same strange clicking from across the room. *Snick-snick-snick*. This time it seemed more familiar, but out of context in the middle of a surgery, like a noise she should somehow recognize but couldn't place. She stood, focused, holding a scalpel in her hand, staring into space and waiting to hear it again.

"Lykke," said Margo. "Are you okay?"

"That clicking. It's been driving me crazy all week."

"What clicking?"

Before either of them could speak, the door to the garage swung open.

"We found your dog," said Timuu, one of the local hunters. They threw on their parkas and followed him outside to an idling snowmobile. The carcass of the dead animal lay on the wooden *qamutiik*, the sled, attached to his snowmobile. Encrusted with ice, the dog's legs stuck out at harsh angles, its gaping abdomen packed with snow. "He was under the hotel."

"We can only hope it was quick," said Lykke, unable to take her eyes off the dog's black eyes gleaming in the winter sun. A chill swept up through her, leaving her suddenly light-headed. "Let's get back to work."

The last surgery of the day was a routine spay, but the procedure was complicated by a pus-filled uterus that needed to be removed. Lykke swooned slightly under the heat of the lamps, having difficulty focusing on the task at hand. The female was in heat, her uterine horns dark red and engorged. Margo stood watch, monitoring the situation and keeping an eye on the vitals. She coughed anxiously, setting Lykke's nerves on edge. Lykke dug into the cavity of the animal, searching for the inflamed horn in order to remove it. *Snick-snick-snick.* This time it was somewhere behind her, and it distracted her momentarily. She seized the offending organ with one hand while reaching for a hemostat to clamp it. Once clamped down, she could sever it and perform the ligate suture. Margo emitted another nervous cough as Lykke placed the hemostat around the uterine horn. In the split second before she released the clamp, Margo thrust a hand into view and shouted, "Wait!"

Lykke, shocked back into reality, looked to Margo for clarification. "That's the duodenum," said Margo, looking sheepish. "I mean, I don't want to interfere, but I'm pretty sure."

Lykke re-examined the situation at her fingertips. It was indeed the wrong organ. An amateur mistake. The animal might have died. She blinked rapidly and tried to focus, composing herself. "Thank you," said Lykke, her voice a whisper, and she pulled the hemostat back from the animal's intestine.

After the surgery, she left Margo behind to clean up and stumbled back to the hotel. In her room, she slipped off her shoes and pulled off her socks, massaging her tired feet with her aching hands. She needed to lie down.

Lykke fumbled for the clock on the nightstand. Nearly four in the morning. With a parched mouth and pounding head, she threw off the bedsheets and dragged her aching body to the bathroom. Her bare feet stung on the frigid hardwood. The harsh light above the mirror blinded her. She threw an arm across her eyes to shield them and flipped off the light. Urinating in the dark, she cradled her head in her hands, resting her elbows on her knees, her mind spiralling into chaos. In an effort to regain control, she tried to recall the mindfulness exercises she'd listened to on the plane. She inhaled, holding it for a count of three and then exhaled, counting again. After several breaths, she felt calmer, less manic. *Better get back in bed*, she thought, *before I can't sleep at all.*

But a steady clicking drew her attention to the door. Her leg muscles seized, locking her in place while she focused on the returning familiar sound. *Snick-snick-snick.* The noises drifted back and forth in the hallway beyond the door. Her mind grasped the nature of the noise—a dog's untrimmed nails on the hardwood floor. She stepped toward the door, light leaking in around it, creating a bright outline of a rectangle in the room, her eyes not yet adjusted to the darkness. Hesitating, she reached for the knob. Before she could grasp it, the smell of isoflurane hit her. It had to be a holdover from her long day in surgery, she thought, traces of the scent lingering in her brain. Or perhaps it had clung to her clothes, hiding in the dirty laundry piled by the dresser. She rubbed her nose as if to clear it of the chemical. There were no dogs in the hotel. This was all in her mind, she told herself. Her feet ached from the cold floor, and she curled her toes, padding from foot to foot, shifting her weight to ease the pain. She gripped her forearm with her opposite hand, digging her nails into the flesh to reassure herself she wasn't still dreaming.

Facing her fear, she braced herself and tore open the door. Left and right, the full length of the corridor was empty and silent. An emergency exit at one end, the doorway to the dining room at the other, and not a soul in between. She stepped out into the hallway, listening for the source of the clicking sound. *A broken thermostat?* she considered. *Or a raven on the hotel roof?* She trod warily down toward the far end of the corridor, toward the door to the dining room. Nothing but shadows and the hum of the appliances in the nearby kitchen.

Satisfied, she re-entered her darkened room. Leaning against the closed door, she heaved a deep breath before rummaging for her pills in her suitcase by the light of the window. Outside, beyond the icy pane, rising wind whipped the blanket of powdered snow around the hotel into whirling eddies taller than the building itself. The power lines swung back and forth in wide arcs in the light of the street lamp. With a resounding bang, a spray of sparks lit up the pole outside the building. The thin line of hallway light bleeding into Lykke's room from beneath the door flickered twice before dying, and the red numbers on her alarm clock blinked out.

In the darkness, without the ambient hums and buzzes of the hotel, the tumult of the storm outside seemed amplified. She'd been in blackouts before. Without power, the furnace would cut out. It likely wouldn't be fixed until tomorrow morning given the weather. Standing in her underwear, Lykke swore she could already feel the cold seeping into her skin. She pulled on a pair of yoga pants and a sweater and crawled back under the covers.

Once tucked in tight, she heard a sound from the hallway that sent shivers through her trembling limbs. *Snick-snick-snick.* She leapt up from the bed and lunged toward the dresser. Rummaging through the top drawer, she found her flashlight. She approached the door and pressed her ear to its surface. Faint whimpering. She listened intently, determined, until a scratching sound drove her scrambling back from the door. She slammed her elbow hard into the wall and cursed in the darkness.

Margo, she thought. It had to be. The young girl was likely fed up with her irritability and drunk on the whiskey she'd taken to bed with her. With her heart racing, Lykke tore open the door, only to find there was nothing in the hallway. Immediately, Lykke knocked on Margo's door, prepared to confront her. No answer. She knocked again, louder. Still nothing. Lykke turned toward the dining area, and the dark space in the doorway at the end of the hall. *She's hiding in the kitchen*, she thought. She steeled herself with a series of deep, nasal breaths, gritted her teeth, and crept toward it.

The flashlight beam cut across the dining room, casting shadows across the unoccupied room. Lykke maneuvered through, trying not to bump into tables and chairs in the dark. Another series of whimpers erupted from a nearby corner and she froze, too terrified to shine the light in its direction. When the noise didn't come a second time, she cast the light on the offending corner and found a door slightly ajar. She approached with caution, shuffling toward it. Shining her light through the thin opening, the furnace and a large water tank were visible. Old paint cans, buckets, and electrical cords littered the floor around them. A gust of wind hammered the hotel; the bones of the old building creaked with the strain of the storm. She pushed the door open wider with her foot. The residual heat from the furnace wrapped around her as she entered.

A lone figure lay slumped against the back wall near the furnace, chin against chest, face obscured by shadows. She approached cautiously, taking one slow step, then a slower second, afraid to cast the beam on the person's face. Words failed her as she considered calling out to the stranger. Pinpricks skittered up her legs, and her ribs seemed to tighten around her lungs. Her third step landed her bare foot in a puddle of water. She lowered her flashlight to reveal a growing pool around the boots of the fallen man. They were boots she recognized, out of place a thousand miles from home. She raised the light upward, illuminating the man in the dark corner, knowing every second exactly who it was, no matter how impossible it seemed.

Michael's body, still dressed in the soaking wet clothes he had drowned in, still wrapped in the rope and anchor, lay before her in the furnace room. The needle, empty of the ketamine it once contained, dangled inconceivably from his neck where she had thrust it. His eyes were open, fixated on her, shining from the flashlight in her trembling hands. His vacant expression brought forth flashes of her dream from the night before. She knelt, her unsteady legs unable to bear her weight any longer.

As she reached out to him, unsure of what part of him to touch, if he was even real, a deep growl erupted from the shadows beside her. In the corner of her vision, two eyes glowed with nightshine not four feet away. Lykke stood carefully, knowing that an angry dog would react to sudden movement, and backed out of the furnace room. She bumped into a table and spun round on impact, whipping the beam of her flashlight around the room. The darkness lit up with a multitude of shining eyes, a chorus of growls and barks breaking out all around her. The dogs of her dreams had almost surrounded her.

In a flood of panic, Lykke turned and fled. Her flailing arms sent several chairs crashing to the ground as she scrambled back across the dining hall. As her feet hit the hallway floor, the pack snarled and snapped at her heels. Breathless and wide-eyed, she grabbed the handle of the door to her room and tried to turn it. It wouldn't budge. Without hesitation, she flung herself farther down the hallway as the dogs tore at her clothing and tried to slow her down. When she reached the end, she turned to face her attackers, and a raging blur of fangs and fur leapt up and struck her in the chest with its powerful frame, sending her bursting out through the emergency door. Lykke tumbled down a long flight of stairs and landed on her back in the drifted snow.

The dogs were gone.

But relief did not last long. She clambered to her feet, the winter air already seeping in through her inadequate clothing. Outside in these temperatures without a parka, she wouldn't last more than half an hour. Her back and ribs felt tender and bruised from the awkward impact on the metal staircase. She scrambled back up the steps and pounded on the steel outer door until her hands burned with the cold. She jammed them into her armpits in a desperate attempt to warm them. Lykke descended the stairs and ran around the side of the building to Margo's window. She climbed the drift toward it, unable to get high enough to see inside, snow biting into her bare feet with a vicious sting. There was nothing small enough around for her to throw at the pane above. The skin on her exposed face burned from the gale-force wind, her legs numb and hands searing with pain. She screamed Margo's name until her voice was hoarse, but the light in her employee's room stayed off.

The churning snowstorm surrounded Lykke in impenetrable whiteness. Wading through the drifting snow toward what she hoped was the entrance to the hotel, she found herself encircled by dark lupine shapes in the swirling maelstrom. She stumbled and fell before crawling beneath the nearest building, out of the wind. She curled into the fetal position, covering her stinging face with her frozen hands. A chorus of low growls surrounded her, advancing inward. She closed her eyes, holding her breath, waiting for death to happen.

When it didn't, she opened her eyes. The dark shapes surged, pinning her on her back. Ravaging snarls and low guttural sounds overwhelmed her. Pain shot through her limbs as she flailed and screamed, trying to protect her face and throat from their snapping jaws. Her screams died on the yowling wind. Warm blood flowed down her neck and back. She felt the hot breath of a dog in her ear before it clamped down on her jugular.

The next morning, two local hunters found Dr. Lykke Jepsen fifteen feet from the main door of the hotel. Her sweater and pants had been removed, cast aside in the snow. Her naked body had been frozen solid, hands positioned below her chin, twisted and turned like the talons of a crippled bird. Her fingernails were caked thick with frozen blood; deep red gouges down her face and torso leapt out from her pale skin. Her eyelids were frosted open, the lashes encrusted with ice. But it was her mouth that most disturbed all who saw her. It gaped wide, slightly wider than anyone would have thought possible, as if poor Lykke had screamed herself to death.

Glossary

Notes on Inuktitut pronunciation

There are some sounds in Inuktitut that may be unfamiliar to English speakers. The pronunciations below convey those sounds in the following ways:

- A double vowel (e.g., aa, ee) lengthens the vowel sound.
- ŋ is a sound similar to the "ng" in the word "sing."
- q is a "uvular" sound, a sound that comes from the very back of the throat. This is distinct from the sound for k, which is the same as a typical English "k" sound (known as a "velar" sound).
- R is a rolled "r" sound.
- ll is a rolled "l" sound.
- Capitalized letters denote the emphasis for each word.

For more Inuktitut pronunciation resources, including audio recordings of these terms, please visit inhabitmedia.com/inuitnipingit

Inuktitut Term	Pronunciation	Meaning
aakuluk	AA-ku-look	dear
Ajai	a-YAI	Whoa
amauti	a-MOW-ti	A woman's parka with a pouch for carrying a child.

Anaana	a-NAA-na	Mother
Anigit!	a-NE-git	Get out!
Anirniq	a-NIR-niq	name
Ataata	a-TAA-ta	Father
atausiq	a-TOW-siq	one
atii	a-TEE	come on
Avani!	A-va-ni	Go away!
Avvajja	av-VAJ-jah	place name
ii	ee	yes
ijiraujaq	e-yi-ROW-yaq	zombie
ijiraujaq qukiqtara	e-yi-ROW-yaq qu-kiq-ta-ra	I shot a zombie.
ijiraujat	e-yi-ROW-yat	zombies
iksarvik	ik-SAR-vik	breakwater
Inu	I-nu	name
Iqsinaqtutalik Piqtuq	IQ-si-naq-TOOQ-ta-lik PIQ-tooq	Haunted Blizzard
Ittuq	IT-tooq	name
Kinngait	KING-ŋa-it	place name
mahsi*	maah-see	thank you
mahsi cho*	maah-see-choh	thank you very much
Markoosie	MAH-koo-see	name

marruuk	maR-RUUK	two
Na acho*	nah ah-choh	Ancient, giant animals that used to roam the earth—"the giant ones."
nanurluk	na-NUR-look	giant polar bear
Niaqunnguup Kuunga	n-ia-qung-ŋuup koo-ŋa	Apex River
niksik	NIK-sik	A hook used to snag a shot seal.
Nuliajuk	nu-LI-a-yook	The name of a spirit that lives at the bottom of the sea and controls the sea mammals.
Panik	PA-nik	Daughter
pingasut	pi-ŋa-SOOT	three
qajaq	QA-yaq	kayak
qallunaaq	qal-lu-NAAQ	a white person
qallunaat	qal-lu-NAAT	white people
qamutiik	qa-mu-TEEK	sled
Qanuikkavit?	qa-nu-IK-ka-vit	What's wrong?
Qanuinngilatit?	qu-nu-ing-ŋi-LA-tit	Are you okay?
qulliq	QUL-liq	seal oil lamp
qunguliit	qu-ŋu-LIIT	mountain sorrel

savikkuvik	sa-vik-ku-VIK	grub box
Sila	SI-la	sky
Siqiniq	si-QI-niq	name
sitamat	SI-ta-mat	four
Taaqtumi	TAAQ-tu-mi	in the dark
taima	TAI-ma	the end
tallimat	TAL-li-mat	five
Tavvaniippit?	tav-va-NEEP-pit	Are you there?
Timuu	ti-MOO	name
Tuavi!	tu-A-VI	Hurry up!
Ulii	u-LEE	name
Utiqtuq	u-TIQ-tooq	returning or going back

* Tłįchǫ term

Contributors

Aviaq Johnston
Aviaq Johnston is a young Inuk author from Igloolik, Nunavut. Her debut novel, *Those Who Run in the Sky*, won the Indigenous Voices Award for Most Significant Work of Prose in English by an Emerging Indigenous Writer in 2018, was a finalist for the 2018 Governor General's Literary Award for Young People's Literature, and was an honour book for the 2018 CODE Burt Awards for First Nations, Inuit, and Métis Literature. Aviaq has also written a children's picture book called *What's My Superpower?* Her second novel, *Those Who Dwell Below*, was published in spring 2019. She lives in Iqaluit, Nunavut.

Cara Bryant (Ann R. Loverock)
Cara Bryant holds a degree in English and Cinema Studies from the University of Toronto. She is a based in Yellowknife, Northwest Territories, where she lives with her husband, two kids, and dog, Jenni.

Gayle Kabloona
Gayle "Uyagaqi" Kabloona is Ukkusiksalingmiut (from the Back River area north of Baker Lake, Nunavut). Now based in Ottawa, she is interested in blending traditional Inuit storytelling with science fiction and magic realism to create alternate realities. Gayle is an urban planner, emerging writer, and multidisciplinary artist with a focus on fibre arts, ceramics, and printmaking.

Jay Bulckaert

Jay Bulckaert grew up in farm-town Ontario, then moved up North in 2001, where he has carved out a career as a filmmaker with his company Artless Collective and founded the mayhem that is the Dead North Film Festival. He lives, hunts, and creates in Yellowknife with his lady and their two cats.

K.C. Carthew

K.C. Carthew is an award-winning filmmaker from Yellowknife, Northwest Territories. Her work across genres tends to feature the landscape as a character and speaks to the ways in which one's relationship with the environment impacts one's well-being.

Rachel and Sean Qitsualik-Tinsley

Rachel and Sean Qitsualik-Tinsley write fiction and educational works that celebrate the secretive world of Arctic cosmology and shamanism. Of Inuit-Cree ancestry, Rachel was born in a tent at the northernmost tip of Baffin Island. Raised as a boy, she learned Inuit survival lore from her father. Eventually, she survived residential school. Rachel specializes in archaic dialects and balances personal shamanic experience with a university education. She has published over 400 articles on culture and language, been shortlisted for several awards, and has enjoyed many years as a judge for Historica Canada's Indigenous Arts & Stories competition. In 2012, she was awarded the Queen Elizabeth II Diamond Jubilee Medal for contributions to Canadian culture. Sean Qitsualik-Tinsley is of Scottish-Mohawk descent and learned a love of nature and stories from his father. He originally trained as an illustrator, but eventually discovered greater aptitude with words, his sci-fi work winning second place in the California-based Writers of the Future contest. Rachel and Sean sweepingly met at the Banff Centre, Alberta, spending subsequent decades as Arctic researchers and consultants. Together, they have published about a dozen books as English originals, along with many shorter works. They are inspired by the "imaginal intelligence" of pre-colonial, Arctic traditions (ancient Inuit and the now-extinct Tuniit). Many such works are found in K-12 schools and universities across Canada and abroad. Their young adult novel of historical fiction, *Skraelings*, won second prize in the Governor General's Literary Awards of 2014 and first prize for the Burt Award of 2015.

Repo Kempt

Repo Kempt spent over fifteen years working as a criminal lawyer in the remote communities of the Canadian Arctic. He is a regular columnist for Litreactor.com and a member of the Horror Writers Association. You can find him on Facebook, Instagram, and Twitter at @repokempt.

Richard Van Camp

Richard Van Camp is an internationally renowned storyteller and bestselling author of twenty-three books. He was born in Fort Smith, Northwest Territories, and is a proud member of the Dogrib (Tłı̨chǫ) Dene Nation. He is the author of *The Lesser Blessed* (Douglas & McIntyre, 1996), a Canadian classic that has been adapted into a feature film with First Generation Films. His new movie is *Three Feathers*, based on his graphic novel with Krystal Mateus. You can visit Richard on Facebook, Twitter, and Instagram.

Thomas Anguti Johnston

Thomas Anguti Johnston grew up moving around the Baffin region of Nunavut and northern Quebec (Nunavik). He now lives in Iqaluit, Nunavut, with his two daughters, Amy and Leah, and his partner Aqattuaq. Anguti has been involved in the Inuit political realm, with the National Inuit Youth Council and Inuit Tapiriit Kanatami. He decided to pursue his passion of filmmaking and writing full-time in 2014 and hasn't looked back. Anguti has received the Nunavut Commissioner's award for youth development and the Diamond Jubilee award for media arts. Anguti is an actor, writer, and film director with a passion for telling Inuit stories.